Ape

BENJAMIN B. BECK

ISBN 978-1-62806-080-5
Library of Congress Control Number 2015958582

Published by Salt Water Media
29 Broad Street, Suite 104
Berlin, MD 21811
www.saltwatermedia.com

The cover image of the chimpanzee is used with written permission by John Ireland, North Carolina Zoo.

Dedicated to

Dian Fossey

1932 - 1985

The mountain gorillas of Rwanda, and possibly of the Democratic Republic of Congo and Uganda as well, would no longer exist without Dian's tenacious commitment to their survival and her underappreciated scientific documentation of their lives. Her heritage includes a Rwandan national commitment to the survival of the country's great apes, so she deserves credit for the survival of the country's chimpanzees as well.

Many have questioned her conservation philosophy and tactics, but none can question her success. She paid with years of despair and isolation, and ultimately with her brutal murder.

Preface and Acknowledgements

This is a story about a community of people and a community of chimpanzees in the tiny and densely populated African country of Rwanda. Monkeys also appear. Chimpanzees are great apes, as are gorillas, bonobos, and orangutans. Chimpanzees, bonobos (a different form of chimpanzee), and gorillas live in Africa; orangutans are Asian. Great apes are larger than monkeys, and have bigger brains and shorter tails than monkeys. I sometimes refer to the chimpanzees as "apes" in the story, which is like calling a Mercedes a "car." Chimpanzees, gorillas, and orangutans are often called "monkeys," but this is scientifically incorrect.

Science tells us that today's chimpanzees and humans last shared a common ancestor about six million years ago. Both have been evolving separately since, but chimpanzees and humans are still similar genetically, anatomically, physiologically, and behaviorally. We are also different in many ways. Chimpanzees are approximately the same size as humans but their brains are considerably smaller. There is no question that chimpanzees are the animals most closely related to humans, but there are questions about how similar we are. The similarities and differences in the intelligence and emotions of chimpanzees and humans are the backdrop of this story.

Many scientists have studied chimpanzee behavior and chimpanzee thinking in the wild and in zoos and laboratories over the past two centuries. Many of their findings have been agglomerated in this story without due credit. I have filled in some plausible but yet undemonstrated chimpanzee

i

capabilities. As a result of 45 years of work with great apes, I have learned never to say "they couldn't do that." I provide an afterword that sorts out the descriptions of chimpanzee behavior and thinking that have been scientifically documented from those that are (at present) exaggerations. Spoiler alert: Don't read the afterword before you read the story.

There are chimpanzees, gorillas, and approximately ten species of monkeys in Rwanda. The gorillas live on the forested sides of the rugged Virunga volcanoes. Thousands of ecotourists have had the good fortune to visit these magnificent beings over the past 25 years, and many others have learned about the gorillas from books, magazines, films, television, and the Internet. Gorilla ecotourism is a leading source of income for Rwanda. The Rwandan chimpanzees are less well known.

The story is set in Rwanda's Gishwati Forest, which is less than 50 miles from the Virunga volcanoes. In 1930, Gishwati covered more than 100 square miles, and large animals like elephants and perhaps gorillas and chimpanzees moved between the two forests. By 2006, Gishwati had been reduced to fewer than 3 square miles, hemmed in on all sides by 850,000 subsistence farmers. In the 1990s, poor and war-scarred Rwandans needed fields to grow their food and graze their cows and goats, so they cut down the trees. They needed wood for cooking and for heat and light, so they cut down more trees. Gishwati's chimpanzees were down to only 13 in 2006, and they were completely cut off from any other chimpanzees.

In September of 2007, His Excellency Paul Kagame, the President of Rwanda, and Ted Townsend, Founder and then Chair of the Great Ape Trust of Iowa, agreed to establish a new national park in Rwanda to protect apes, improve the livelihoods of Rwandans, and promote global environmental health. The Gishwati remnant was chosen as the site of the new park. The forest and its chimpanzees are now recovering and expanding, and Gishwati has recently become a fully protected national park.

I am indebted to President Kagame and Mr. Townsend for their vision. Ted invested millions in the Gishwati effort over the following five years, and asked me to head the Trust's conservation program during that time. Were it not for him, this would likely be a story of extinction.

I am deeply grateful to the citizens of the four sectors of Rutsiro district that include Gishwati who, despite interests that often conflict with those of conservationists, gave us a chance to show that conservation would indeed improve their lives in the long run. I hope we kept our promises.

We selected Madeleine Nyiratuza to be the Rwandan coordinator of the Gishwati program. Mado is zealously but realistically dedicated to environmental conservation. She is strategic, firm, tactful, tireless, and has a wry sense of humor. I benefitted from her wise counsel and encouragement.

Our Rwandan team also included Simeon Habyarimana, Sylvain Nyandwi, Marshall Banamwana, Thomas Safari, Samuel Uwimana, Jean Damascene Uwanyirijuru, Alexis Ruzindana, Etienne Gasominari, Christian Rugero, Patience

Mwiseneza, Edison Kabenga, Alexis Ndayambaje, Olivier Ngabonziza, Etienne Munyabirori, Edison Kamende, Faustin Gashakamba, Robert Rwanuma, Emmanuel Hubumugisha, Eric Munyeshuri, Hadidja Nyiraminani, and some trail cutters whose names I never recorded.

Many other Rwandan government officials, educators, and scientists contributed to the success of the work that stimulated this story. I list them here in alphabetical order, with gratitude and vivid memories: Felicia Akinyemi, Nsengiyunva Barakabuye, Augustin Basabose, Christophe Bazivamo, Phillipe Gasarisa, Patricia Hajabakiga, Stanislas Kamanzi, Juliet Kabera, Rose Kabuye, James Kimonyo, Silas Lwakabamba, Michel Masozera, Tony Mudakikwa, Adrie Mukashema, Rose Mukankomeje, Therese Musabe, Jean Ndimubahire, Telesphore Ngoga, Jean-Damascene Nsanzimfura, Rosette Rugamba, Louis Rugerinyange, Frank Rutabingwa, Eugene Rutagarama, Fidele Ruzigandekwe, Karolina Uwantege, Fidele Uwimana, and Prosper Uwingeli.

Ex-pat colleagues include Perry Beeman, Glenn Bush, Elizabeth Chadri, David Courard-Hauri, Mike Cranfield, Virginia Croskery, Katie Fawcett, Eberhard Fischer, Julie Ghrist, Charlene Jendry, Beth Kaplin, Annette Lanjouw, Linda May, Martin O'Hara, Jan Ramer, Michael Renner, Aaron Rundus, and Keith Summerville.

I am especially grateful to our Principal Investigator, Rebecca Chancellor, who dedicated three years to the rigorous study of the Gishwati chimpanzees and their forest home.

Peter Clay, a colleague at the Great Ape Trust in Iowa,

brought decades of ape experience in Africa (including Rwanda, where he had worked with Dian Fossey) and in zoos to our work in Gishwati. I am indebted to Peter for his expertise, thoughtful counsel, and unbending ethics.

Other Trust colleagues who contributed directly to our work are Al Setka, Dana Vastine Watson, Casie Pitman, Beth Dalbey, Susan Mc Kee, Rob Shumaker, Kristina Walkup, and Serge Wich.

Patty Gregorio provided expertise on the capabilities of an iPhone 5c, and Mike Price, Will Moore, Jonathan King, Sean Thistle, and Dean Peterland of the Maryland State Police Aviation Command were generous with their time and encouragement while showing me the workings of helicopter-based ground surveillance.

Judith Block, Karen Bonnin, Peter Clay, Chris Engen, and Madeleine Nyiratuza provided helpful comments and suggestions on the manuscript.

My editor, Stephanie Fowler, critically reviewed the manuscript and guided the process at Salt Water Media with a skilled, firm, and empathetic hand.

I am most grateful to my wife Beate who managed our responsibilities and handled some difficult family challenges during my long trips to Rwanda. She also read the manuscript and endured lapses of my attention during the writing.

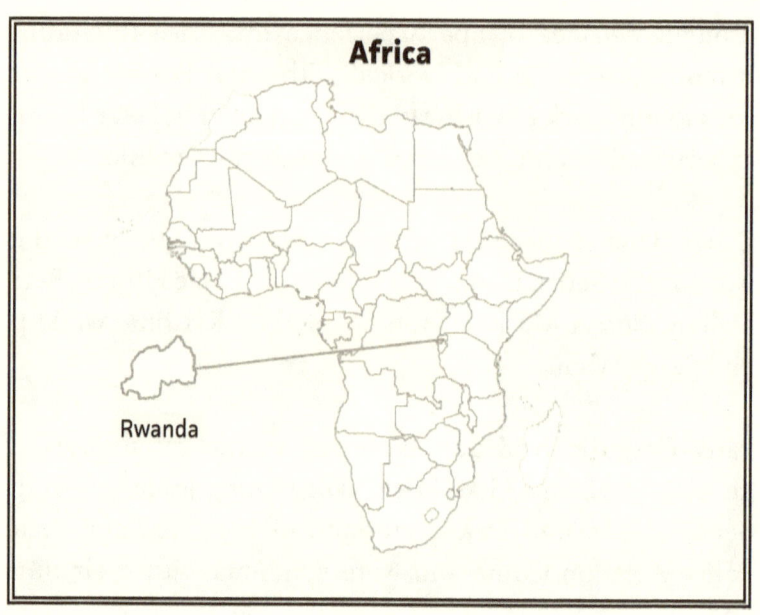

Africa

Rwanda

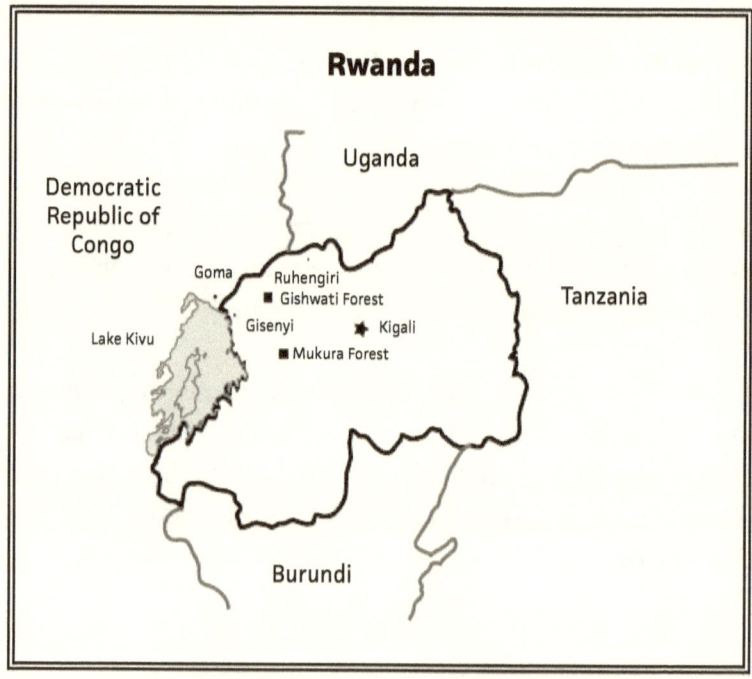

Rwanda

Uganda

Democratic
Republic of
Congo

Goma

Ruhengiri
■ Gishwati Forest

Gisenyi
★ Kigali

Lake Kivu

■ Mukura Forest

Tanzania

Burundi

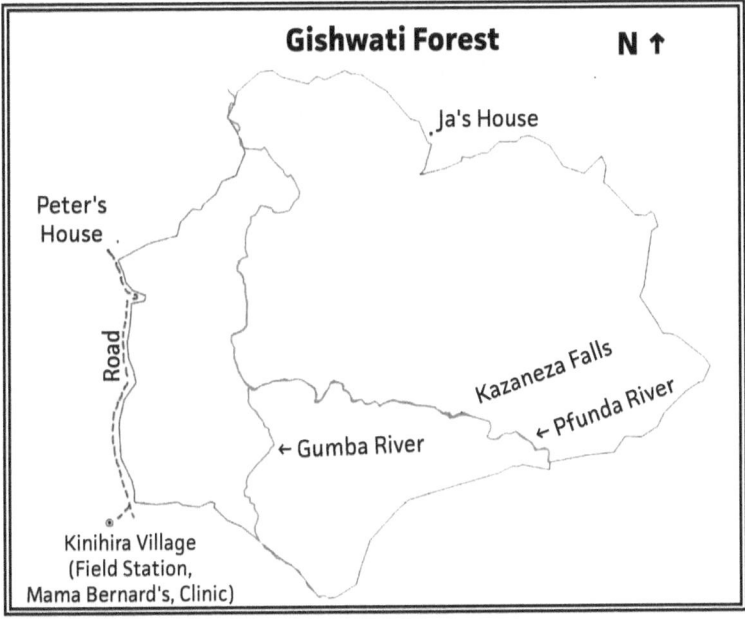

Chapter 1) Salt Lick

The chimpanzee known as Mango sat motionless on his haunches on a thick limb, 50 feet up in a towering old tree. Even his brown eyes were still as they fixed on the steep hillside below. He was well fed, but today he was craving salt. The women below stood shoulder-to-shoulder in a cross-slope line, hoeing the thick brown clay. Their brows glistened with sweat as they swung their hoes and gossiped.

One hundred feet upslope, on a flat grassy clearing near Mango's tree, six of their infants, swaddled in bright fabric, lay on sheets, sleeping or gurgling in contentment. Mango was calculating slope and speed, and decided to make his move.

He descended soundlessly and was undetected until he broke from the tree line into the clearing. He reached the babies just as the women began their screaming, upslope scramble. He picked up a baby and shook it. The baby remained stoically silent. Mango dropped her. The other babies now began to wail. Mango eagerly licked the tears that rolled down their chubby brown cheeks, going from infant to infant, like a bee searching flowers for nectar. The adults were soon within 30 feet, menacing with waving hoes. Mango stopped slurping and disappeared as quietly as he had arrived.

Chapter 2) Tears

Stone, the chimpanzee group's leader, was waiting for Mango in the forest. Stone was angry. At Mango's approach,

Stone stood upright, rocking sideways from foot to foot, his hair erect. His soft hoots grew to fearsomely loud staccato screams, and then he charged Mango, slamming the side of his head with a muscled arm and biting him in the shoulder.

Mango screamed and retreated. Stone sat on the ground and ate some leaves from a shrub. After a few quieting minutes, Mango began to inch closer to Stone, carefully avoiding direct eye contact. As he got close, Mango extended his arm, palm up, and pulled back his lips, showing his teeth. Humans would call this a smile but for chimpanzees it is a gesture of fear and respect. Stone, after all, was the alpha male of the Gishwati Forest chimpanzee group, and Mango wanted to make up.

Mango liked to touch and smell human babies when he could and had discovered that this made them cry. He liked the taste of their salty tears and had begun to handle the babies roughly to make them cry. He found that licking baby tears was an exciting alternative to getting needed salt by eating dirt in Clay Cave, which was the custom of the Gishwati chimpanzees.

Stone was soon lying on the ground with Mango grooming him, picking through his hair for scabs, bits of dead skin, and the occasional parasite. Stone was cleaner as a result but the real purpose of this grooming bout was to allow these two powerful males to make peace. As he relaxed under Mango's touch, Stone was thinking about why Mango shook babies and licked their faces. In all of his 40-plus years, he had never known another chimpanzee who tried to handle human babies. Because chimpanzees don't cry or shed tears, he also didn't know that human tears were salty.

Stone did know that he would have to eject Mango from the group if he continued to handle human babies. The people of Gishwati would not tolerate such behavior much longer. Stone's group had to coexist with these people because there was no other forest nearby. If the people began to hunt them, there would be no other place for the apes to go and not enough food to eat. Mango's deviance would doom them all.

Carrot, a beautiful young female chimpanzee, sat down and joined Mango in grooming Stone. Stone had shared some of the meat from this morning's monkey kill with Carrot. Both Stone and Mango liked to mate with her when she was receptive, and she knew how to stay on the good side of these males and how to influence their decisions. The tension subsided.

Chapter 3) Dr. Alicia

Dr. Alicia Oliveira awoke to rain pounding on the corrugated metal roof of the Gishwati Chimpanzee Project field station. She had slept in sweat pants and a sweatshirt during the cold humid night, and now kept them on as she trudged through the yard in the pre-dawn light to the small clay building that enclosed the pit latrine. When she was done, she washed up and brushed her teeth at the outdoor faucet and returned to her small, sparsely furnished room. She could smell the smoky fire and knew that Leonard, her cook, was brewing coffee and making oatmeal. Her lithe and muscled body rippled as she pulled on layers of rip-stop field clothes, thick socks and slippers. Months of following chimpanzees up and down the steep hills of the Gishwati Forest had melted every ounce of extra fat from her body and honed her aerobic fitness.

"Good morning Dr. Alicia," said Leonard, as she walked into the field station's small dining room. "Here's your coffee. I'll bring the oatmeal in a minute. Honey or strawberry jam this morning?"

The nearest market was 30 miles away, and the field station had no electricity or refrigeration. Alicia ate the whole week on what could be driven up the mile-high mountain on once-a-week shopping trips to the city below. The choice of honey or jam to put on her morning oatmeal was a bright moment in an otherwise monotonous diet.

"Honey this morning, please."

Chapter 4) Peter

Peter Kabera, Alicia's field assistant, came into the dining room carrying a small can of still-warm milk that he had purchased five minutes earlier from a farmer at the edge of Kinihira village, in which the field station was located. He gave the milk to Leonard, bid Dr. Alicia good morning, folded his dripping umbrella, and carefully removed his wet rain jacket before sitting down at the table.

As always, Alicia was warmed by Peter's politeness and good manners. Peter had been two when his parents had built a clay house nearby, on the edge of what remained of the vast

Gishwati Forest, in 1994. They were refugees of Rwanda's violent civil war. Peter attended elementary school but his family could not afford to send him to high school. He had taught himself English and read every book he could get his hands on. He made a little money by tending cows and cleaning the local mission school. His passion, starting in his pre-teens, was the forest and the animals and plants that lived there. He spent every spare moment walking in the forest. He knew when different kinds of trees would have flowers and fruit, when the bamboo sprouted, and where the chimpanzees and the monkeys traveled and slept. He could identify the birds and reptiles, but had only recently learned their English and scientific names from Dr. Alicia's books.

When Dr. Alicia had appeared a year ago to begin a long-term study of the Gishwati chimpanzees, Peter was an obvious choice to become her field assistant. He was also a powerful ambassador for her in Kinihira and the surrounding rural community.

"There was another baby-shaking yesterday afternoon," said Peter.

Leonard set down a steaming bowl of *igikoma*, a local porridge-like breakfast staple made of the fresh cow's milk and corn, sorghum and soy flour. It was soupier than Alicia's oatmeal, but would see Peter through an arduous morning of walking up and down steep hills in the cold rain. Peter added a little honey.

"Anybody hurt?" asked Alicia.

"No, but the people are angry."

"Who was it?" asked Alicia.

"They described an adult male, so it's either Stone, Fig, Chicken, or Mango. He was all black, so it wasn't Stone."

The Gishwati chimpanzee group now had 21 members. Four were adult males. Peter had first recognized and named these males 10 years ago, when he himself was 12. The hair on Stone's chin and above his lips had already started to turn gray then. Peter thought Stone was now around 40. Fig, Chicken and Mango had been juveniles when Peter had met them. That would make them between about 20 now. The hair on their faces was still mostly black but their chins were graying. They were still subordinate to Stone, who kept them in line and rarely had to resort to a serious beating.

Chapter 5) The Follow

"Who's our follow today?" asked Alicia.

"Apple and Bee," answered Peter.

Alicia and Peter could not study all 21 chimpanzees every day. The apes don't stay together as a group all the time. Even if they did, two observers could not collect detailed data on all of the animals simultaneously. The observers needed to focus. The "follow" was the chimpanzee whose movement and behavior Alicia and Peter would study today.

The chimpanzee follow of the day had been chosen randomly,

weeks earlier. If Alicia studied the most interesting animals each day, such as the males that were fighting to move up in the dominance hierarchy, or the females who were ready to mate, or the males that were hunting monkeys, or the ones who were currently using tools to dig honey out of underground bee nests, she would get an unrealistic, overly dramatic picture of chimpanzee life. Life would be all aggression, hunting, sex and tool use, which were all subjects of great interest to scientists and the public. But the chimpanzees spent a lot of their time quietly eating leaves and fruits, resting, grooming, and caring for their babies, activities that are far less exciting yet crucial to chimpanzee life. By following a randomly chosen chimpanzee every day, Alicia could capture both the exciting and unexciting events in accurate proportions.

"We should probably keep an eye on the males," said Peter.

"The folks won't be leaving their babies out in the rain... no baby-shaking today," said Alicia.

She blew out the candle as the first light came through the small dining room window, and slipped into her rain suit, traded her slippers for boots, grabbed her pack, and headed for the field station gate, with Peter a stride behind.

Chapter 6) Meat Market

The city of Gisenyi is 30 miles from the Gishwati Forest. It sits on the shore of Lake Kivu, one pearl in the north-to-south necklace of central Africa's Great Lakes. The mostly unpaved road from Gishwati drops 2,500 feet to the city, and many travelers end up at the bus station on Umuganda Avenue. It's a dusty and chaotic place, fronted by a garish blue and white, Samsung-branded, three story building that houses the ticket office and Madam Chen's dark, closet-sized store on the ground floor.

Madam Chen's age was elusive. She always wore a shirt with a Mao-style collar that hung loosely over a strikingly colored piece of African cloth that was wrapped around the lower half of her short, chubby body. She wore a black wool watch cap, pulled tightly over her cropped, graying hair. The outfit made her shapeless, and shabby running shoes rounded out her charmless persona. She smelled of mildew and soy sauce.

Madam Chen stood, barely visible, behind her overstocked counter for 18 hours a day, selling gum, candy, crackers, cookies, cans of Fanta, bottles of water, and cards for buying cellphone minutes. For a few familiar and wealthier customers, she would slip into a back room and bring out a leg of heavily smoked antelope or monkey or other illegal bushmeat, wrapped in newspaper.

She was at the moment talking quietly to two grimy men who were part of her network of illegal hunters: "Bring me a live baby chimpanzee and I'll give you one thousand dollars U.S. I can get it shipped to China, but I need you to get me the ape."

"Impossible," said one of the men. "They're difficult to catch, and there are guards in the forests. These days, even the police will lock you up if they catch you with a chimp or gorilla."

"One thousand dollars U.S. for a live baby chimp," she repeated. The men were used to snaring antelopes and monkeys for a dollar or two each day. A thousand was a fortune. "I hear there are hundreds of them in Nyungwe," she said. "They sleep in nests at night. You should be able to get one."

"Nyungwe is a national park and it's crawling with tourists and scientists... and guards," answered one of the men.

"There are chimps at Gishwati," said the other. "I used to live there. There's only one guy who keeps an eye on the forest, and he's not even paid."

"Bring me a chimp, a baby," Madam Chen said. "Or should I find somebody else to do it?"

"Will you throw in a couple of shotgun shells?"

Chapter 7) Feedback

Thirty Kinihira residents waited for Dr. Alicia and Peter as they walked out of the gate. The rain had turned the street into stony mud and puddles. The women were soaked and angry.

"You have to make them stop," said one of the women, in Kinyarwanda, the Rwandan native tongue. Peter translated for Alicia.

"I can't control them," she said, through Peter.

"You can look from the sky and see what we do," said the woman. She was referring to satellite photos that Dr. Alicia had shown the villagers on her computer on leisurely Sunday afternoons. "You can see our laundry hanging outside our houses, and you could see that my husband was cutting trees on the edge of the forest."

"It doesn't work in the forest," explained Alicia. "The trees are too thick. The camera can't see through them. I can't see the chimpanzees from the sky."

Google Earth had created a huge conceptual shift among the people of Kinihira, none of whom had ever looked down from an airplane. They could look down into valleys, but they couldn't look through the hills to the next valley. The satellite photos showed it all, just by zooming in and out.

"It's bad enough when the chimpanzees eat our corn and avocados, but now they scare our babies. Why does this one shake our babies? This has never happened before."

"I know. I agree that it's bad. I promise I will try to find a solution," said Alicia.

Alicia was thinking along the lines of organizing a day care center for the babies while the women worked in the fields. She did not realize at that moment just how complicated the solution would be.

One of the few men in the crowd mumbled: "We'll have to

shoot him." Peter did not translate this.

Chapter 8) Apple and Bee

Apple was about 20, and Bee, now 19 months old, was her second infant. Bee was still nursing on Apple but was also sampling some of the leaves and fruits that her mother was eating. Apple still carried Bee and cuddled her in her nest each night, but Bee had begun to climb around in branches near Apple. When Apple and her companions stopped to rest on the ground, Bee sought out Potato, the only other youngster her age in the Gishwati group. Bee and Potato would gently wrestle and tickle each other under the watchful eyes of their mothers and the other group members. They would be retrieved quickly if they wandered too far, and corrected if their play got too rough.

Peter had watched Apple build her nest last evening. She broke and bent branches to make a body-sized bowl up in a tree, and lined it with leaves. He knew that each adult chimpanzee made a new nest each evening.

Peter and Alicia arrived at Apple's nest at 6:30 a.m. after 22 minutes of brisk walking. Alicia walked a little faster than usual, unconsciously trying to put some distance between her and the angry mothers. The log over the Gumba River had not washed away and still provided a bridge for a dry crossing. Having arrived at the nests, Peter and Alicia leaned against tree trunks and looked up, the rain stinging their eyes.

"There they are, getting up right on time," said Alicia. She peered through binoculars. "Definitely Apple, and she's got the baby," said Alicia. "I'll call, you write," she added, handing Peter an aluminum case that contained the data collection sheets.

Peter had taught Alicia to identify each of the 21 chimpanzees. At first, they would look at the conspicuous sex organs to see if the ape was a male or female and then used body size to narrow the possibilities. The color of the facial skin, which varied from black to gray to pink, with distinctive pink spots on black skin or black spots on pink skin almost always allowed individual identification. Graying hair, scars, tattered ears, and missing fingers and toes were also valuable clues. Now, after months of observation, Alicia, like Peter, knew each of the chimpanzees at a glance.

"I guess I should have been more sympathetic, but it's hard when you don't speak the language," said Alicia.

"I'll talk to them again tonight," said Peter. "They're more scared than angry, and this baby-licking chimp, whoever he is, is really dangerous."

"Can you shoot a gun?" she asked.

"No, can you?"

"No."

"Would you...?" Peter began to ask, but had to stop because Alicia was dictating her observations.

Other chimpanzees were arising from their nests. They stopped to poop and pee, and then moved out. They never fouled their nests. Today they headed for the big bamboo grove. Alicia noted where Apple's feces had landed and quickly scooped a sample into a plastic jar. There would be powerful information extracted later from that bit of waste.

Chapter 9) Ja

Ja appeared suddenly and soundlessly next to Peter and Alicia. He was barefoot, and wore tattered khaki shorts and a faded, oversized blue sweatshirt that read "Josh Greenberg's Bar Mitzvah, 1999." That shirt had traveled from a used clothing drive in Houston to a mission on the Gishwati mountainside for distribution to poor Rwandans. Nobody in Kinihira understood the English writing on Ja's shirt, not even the teacher, who had an English-Kinyarwanda dictionary. Ja didn't care what it said; he was happy to have a warm shirt.

Ja was only 5'6" tall, slender, and wiry. He had short, graying hair and a stubbly beard that never seemed to grow. He carried a long, stained machete. His eyes were chronically bloodshot from indoor cooking fires and a good share of banana beer.

Ja was a Batwa, which is a tribal name in a vast nation of small-statured hunter-gatherers who had populated these forests of central Africa for tens of thousands of years. They had been nomads, at peace with their world, hunting small animals, collecting fruits, mushrooms, eggs, snails, insects, and honey, and building temporary huts of limbs and leaves.

The Batwa and the chimpanzees had shared the forest and respected each other. Sometimes they competed for honey or other staples, but each took only what they needed and left plenty for the other. The chimpanzees watched the Batwa carefully as the people hunted, socialized, raised their babies, built their huts, and donned and shed the few clothes that they wore.

In the Past Times, before the Europeans arrived, there were more similarities than differences between these people and the apes. Both made and used wooden and stone tools, although the Batwa had also been trading for metal tools for two millennia. Both hunted monkeys, rodents, and small antelopes, but the Batwa used nets, snares, spears, and bows with poison-tipped arrows. The chimpanzees used stealth, speed, and strength. Both suffered stings when they raided wild beehives for honey, but the Batwa built fires and used smoke to chase off some of the bees. Batwa huts kept out the rain, but chimpanzee nests had no tops and they relied on their long, silky hair to stay dry.

Batwa men could climb trees, but they only went up and down the trunks and could not travel from tree to tree on the branches. Chimpanzees could travel effortlessly through the tops of the trees. On the other hand, the Batwa could walk on two legs for miles on the ground while they carried things in their hands and on their heads. The chimpanzees traveled on all fours on the ground, and could not carry very much very far.

The biggest difference was that the Batwa spoke to each other with words, and could arrange their words into long, meaningful sentences. They could talk about the location of faraway caves, last year's landslide, the way to make beer, and a hunt that was being planned for the night. They gossiped about naughty little secrets. The chimpanzees had listened carefully for millennia but had never been able to learn more than a few words, and they could not speak these clearly out loud. Sometimes the chimpanzees sat in a tree at the edge of the forest near the Kinihira school and listened to the reverberating voices of teachers and students through the glassless windows as they sang and recited their lessons.

The Europeans who colonized Africa were especially disrespectful of the Batwa, whom they regarded as the most primitive of the primitive Africans. Now, even other Africans ridiculed, marginalized, and persecuted the Batwa. The local Batwa clan had been resettled (some would say evicted) from the Gishwati Forest when it had been made a reserve, and there was no other forested area in which they could continue their traditional lives. The Rwandan government built lovely clay houses with corrugated metal roofs and sturdy doors for each of the eleven families in the clan. The Batwa fled in terror when they first heard rain hammering on the tin roofs. Rain, they thought, should make a gentle sound. They built traditional huts instead, and sold the corrugated metal and the doors. They tried to farm but lacked the knowledge and the will. A few of the children went to the local school, but they struggled with books because they had no tradition of the written word. Only one student was currently enrolled. The Batwa snuck back into the forest to hunt and gather. Peter and the chimpanzees knew of these intrusions but neither objected. It was the last remnant of the Past Times.

Peter had suggested to Dr. Alicia that she hire Batwa men to cut and maintain trails in the forest. He cautioned her that they are not the most reliable and punctual of workers, but assured her that nobody was better qualified when it came to trails. They knew how to find the best routes and how to build trails that would not wash away in tropical deluges.

Ja was glad to have a job that paid the equivalent of 50 cents a day plus lunch and a uniform and boots (for which he saw no need). Alicia was happy to give Ja a job, and the foundation that supported her work was pleased that she shared their sense of social justice.

Chapter 10) Bee's Knees

"They're headed for the bamboo," said Alicia as she screwed the top on the tube containing the fecal sample and slipped it into her backpack. "Let's go."

Ja turned and wordlessly led the way, skillfully slicing overhanging limbs and removing fallen branches from the foot-wide path.

They could see Apple, who was carrying Bee; Potato, who was being carried by his mother Squash; Rain, who was Bee's older sister; and Carrot. The chimpanzees moved effortlessly through the branches. The three field workers marched through the misty forest on the path below. They descended into the valley where the Pfunda River flowed through its rocky riverbed and thundered over the Kazaneza waterfall. The river was swollen from the night's rain, but one could still see the rocky bottom through the brown-green water. Further down the mountain, after the river broke out of the forest and ran through treeless agricultural fields, the water would turn a murky coffee brown as it carried tons of topsoil to Lake Kivu below.

Tree crowns bridged the river here, making the overhead crossing easy for the apes. The people had to cross the swollen river by stepping or jumping from one round and slippery rock to another. Peter and Alicia picked their way across. Ja just strolled.

The apes were already on the ground and had begun to eat when the observers arrived at the bamboo grove. The bamboo sprouted new shoots from the ground for several months each year. The sprouts were greatly prized by the chimpanzees. They would pull a sprout from the ground, tear away the tough outer layers with their fingers and teeth, and eat the sweet, white, juicy pith within.

Peter and Alicia each leaned against a tree trunk. Ja sat on the ground and somehow managed to fall sleep in the rain. Alicia counted each sprout that Apple pulled, the number of outer layers that she removed, and the time it took her to eat each sprout. She dictated the information to Peter, who recorded it on a data sheet. Boring work, but Alicia's grant was targeted to finding out how 21 chimpanzees could find enough to eat in this tiny forest. This question was important for discovering what chimpanzees need to survive.

Bee spent her morning on or near Apple. She nursed for a while (16 minutes on the left nipple and three on the right, as recorded by Alicia and Peter), and snoozed. The rain stopped and the sun tried to break through the low-lying clouds. Bee picked up a small twig and ran a few feet toward Potato, who was sampling Squash's heart of bamboo shoot. As Bee ran past Potato, the little guy grabbed the twig. Bee turned and grabbed Potato around the shoulders, wrestling him to the ground. They squirmed and tussled, each with their mouths open and "laughing" a breathy "*heh...heh... heh...heh*". There were flashes of the pink faces, pink ears, and the white tail tufts that mark chimpanzee infancy from the front, sides, and the back. Bee broke free and dashed for the far side of a nearby tree. Potato followed, and Bee circled the tree, staying just out of his reach. She jumped up and grabbed an overhanging branch, and Potato grabbed her legs to pull her down. He couldn't, so he too jumped up in the tree where they wrestled for possession of this branch as if it were the only branch around. Bee plopped off the branch to the ground, landing next to Rain.

Rain started to tickle her little sister behind the knees, which caused Bee to explode in gleeful laughter. She broke away but quickly returned for more. Rain gripped her by the leg and tickled her again behind the knees until Bee couldn't bear it anymore. Potato felt ignored. Bee was his only playmate in this small group, although sometimes the two youngsters could get Stone and the other males to play with them. Stone knew the behind-the-knees trick too, and enjoyed sending Bee into spasms of laughter. But now, Rain had all of Bee's attention. Potato gave Bee a jealous whack across the neck, and Bee began to scream. Apple and Squash dropped their bamboo shoots and rushed over to intervene. Bee jumped onto Apple's belly and began to nurse. Apple reassured her with gentle pats and soft grunts. Potato tried to scamper away but Squash grabbed him roughly by a hind leg, and put him on her back, jockey-style. Everybody went back to eating, until Bee began to sneak toward Potato another time.

"Where's the boys?" asked Alicia.

"Awfully quiet today," answered Peter. "Maybe they're going to hunt."

"They got that monkey yesterday," said Alicia. "Poor monkey."

"It's all food," observed Peter. "That's why we're here, right?"

Chapter 11) The Chimpanzee Meat Market

Chimpanzee males are noisy. They call, hoot, scream, and pound on trees when they are excited, when they are having sex with an estrous female, when they see a snake, or when they find a tree of ripe fruit. Sometimes they make a racket just to let the world know they're alive. The only times the males are quiet are when they are asleep, have their mouths full of food, are being groomed by an obliging female, or when they are scheming.

Today they were scheming. They were making a plan, not unlike Madam Chen and her hired poachers. The apes sat silently and motionless on the ground, watching a group of mountain monkeys feed in the trees above. Mountain monkeys are cocker spaniel-sized, gray monkeys with a very long tail, a striking collar of bright white hair and flashes of bright white below their eyes. They live in groups of 10 to 50 and stay mostly in the treetops. They walk and climb on all fours, and can't jump far, a fact of biology that the chimpanzees exploited.

Chimpanzees eat mainly fruit, leaves, flowers, and pith but they are not vegetarians. They also eat birds' eggs, ants, bees, and honey when they can, and turn to larger prey, especially monkeys, to fill their needs for other vitamins and minerals.

It is not easy to catch a monkey. The chimpanzee strategy involves one or two males driving a monkey toward a gap in the forest canopy that is too wide for the monkey to jump across. Others chimpanzees block the monkey's escape to the side, and still others wait below the gap. When the monkey gets to the gap, it can run back the way it came or drop to the ground below. Either way, a chimpanzee will be waiting.

Scientists argue whether male chimpanzees really do plan and cooperate in a hunt, or whether each animal acts independently in a way that is likely to get him the prize. The consensus is that there is a plan and that they do cooperate. In any case, it's clear that a chimpanzee hunting alone would rarely catch a monkey. Of course, when they hunt as a team, they have to share the prey when they do succeed.

Now, the only movement from below was hair bristling on the backs of the four males as they watched the monkeys feed on figs at the edge of the river. There was a gap above the river where the branches didn't touch. The river was wide here, so the gap was too wide to jump. The "boys" had picked their spot.

Stone finally screamed, and he, Chicken, and Fig, also screaming, bolted quickly up into the fig tree. Mango, also screaming and hooting, ran across the ground down into the bottom of the valley and took up station below the gap. The monkeys screamed and scattered, but some ran toward the river. Stone, Chicken, and Fig, 30 feet apart, charged behind them, herding and driving them toward the gap. One monkey avoided the charge and escaped to the left. Another dropped 20 feet into a smaller tree below. Another, an old female, was slower and was being driven fatefully to the gap. The chimpanzees' screaming reached a deafening volume.

"They're hunting," said Peter, quickly putting away the data sheets. The observers knew what was to unfold. So did the bamboo-eating apes, and the observers knew that Apple and Bee, their "follow" for the day, would head to the spot. Rain and Carrot were already on their way up the valley toward the Pfunda on the other side. Apple, carrying Bee, and Squash, with Potato, were close behind. The observers had to follow a more circuitous route. When they arrived, all 21 chimps were at the kill and screaming.

The end was not pretty, painless, or fast enough for the monkey. Now her lifeless body was being pulled and chewed into ever-smaller pieces, first by the four hunters and then by the lucky recipients of their sharing. The adult female chimpanzees approached the males, palms up, arms outstretched, whimpering softly. Stone shared bits of meat readily, first with the adult females and then with begging juvenile males and females. Mango was more selfish, but he did give a piece to Carrot.

"I think the males give meat to the females in exchange for sex later on," said Peter, as they logged the sharing data.

"It looks like that but I read a report last year that combined all of the meat-sharing data from all of the chimpanzee field sites in Africa, and females had sex just as often with selfish males as with sharing males, said Alicia in a professorial tone. "And sharing males had sex just as often with females with whom they had not shared as with females with whom they *had* shared."

"Maybe the ones they share with will groom them or support them in fights," said Peter.

"Nope, same thing," answered Alicia.

Things were calming down. Stone had broken open the monkey's skull and wiped out the last bits of blood and brains with a leafy sponge. He put the whole sponge in his mouth, combined it with some last bits of flesh, and chewed it slowly. Scientists call this mouthful a "wadge". Apple was nibbling and picking the meat off a hand that Fig had given her, and Bee was sniffing her mouth. Bee moved over to Stone, who was reclining on a thick limb and still savoring his wadge. Bee approached cautiously, stretching out her tiny hand. Apple watched attentively, but she knew that Stone loved Bee. Stone thought he was Bee's father, but many males had mated with Apple when she had been receptive. Alicia knew that Stone was indeed Bee's father, based on the DNA that she had retrieved months ago from their feces, but there was no way she could share this finding with Stone.

Bee inched closer and leaned in to smell Stone's mouth. He chewed and turned the wadge in his mouth, and gently pushed Bee away with the back of his forearm. Bee was undeterred, and this time pulled Stone's upper lip back with her fingers, exposing his huge canine teeth. Stone obligingly opened his mouth and let Bee reach in and get a bit of the delicacy.

Alicia narrated: "1331 hours, Bee gets a piece of Stone's wadge."

"But you are on to something, Peter. My boss in Brazil worked at the zoo in Washington D.C., and he said that the zoo apes traded things all the time. If an ape got, say, a rake that a keeper left near the cage, he would pull it into the cage and then trade it for some food, like a piece of a banana. One time, an orangutan used a stick to get a big light bulb from a fixture in the hallway outside the cage. The keepers were especially anxious to get that back, but the orang wouldn't settle for a banana. They had to give her a popsicle."

"What's a popsicle?"

"Like sorbet, frozen sorbet, on a stick. Apes love them."

"So the apes knew that the light bulb was worth more than the rake?" asked Peter.

"Seems like that. And stones. They'd find them in their outdoor yard and bring them inside. Big trading item because they could crack the glass windows of their cages with the stones. The keepers finally had to pick up all of the stones in the yard. The apes started digging more up and even breaking pieces of concrete off the building. The apes actually started a business, trading stones to the keepers for fruit."

"And here's another case," she continued. "A little boy fell into an exhibit at Brookfield Zoo in Chicago about 15 years ago. He was knocked unconscious by the fall. A mother gorilla picked the little boy up and took him to the keepers. Some say it was an act of compassion, but she had been trained with food rewards to bring her own baby to the keepers so they could check it. She knew how to trade looks at her own baby for food, and maybe she was just trading the little boy for food."

"So are you saying that our chimps trade meat for sex?"

"I'm just saying that it's possible. We'll need more data. Maybe they're just not giving away big-enough pieces of meat or the best parts."

Many of the chimps were sucking on wadges now, and the mood had calmed. Bee and Potato were nursing. Many of the older apes, and Ja, were napping. The mountain monkeys were nowhere to be seen.

"I'm going to head back," said Alicia. "Call me on the radio if you need help. Track Apple and Bee until they bed down.

I'll see you in the morning."

Alicia needed a few afternoon hours each day to file her data, store fecal samples properly, and answer her e-mails. There was no electricity in the village of Kinihira. Solar panels on the field station roof provided just enough power to charge the batteries of the two-way radios they used in the forest, her computer, and her cell phone. There was never cell phone coverage in the forest; the valleys were too deep and the tree canopies were too dense. But she could get a connection on most days from the field station.

The best part of these late afternoons was her shower in the closet-sized clay brick stall that adjoined the latrine. Leonard warmed water over the fire and would bring two buckets to the shower stall as Alicia went to her room and pulled off her field clothes. In the stall, she poured one bucket over herself, soaped up her body, and washed her hair. Then she rinsed with the other bucket, and dried herself with a soft towel that she had brought from Brazil. She'd slip into sweat pants and a sweatshirt in anticipation of the cool mountain evening. Leonard would quickly wash her field clothes and start them drying, which, depending on the weather, could take up to 24 hours. But there would always be a clean and neatly folded set of layers for the following morning.

Leonard brought her some freshly ground Rwandan coffee, a small pot of boiling water, and her French coffee press. Alicia had bought the press at the Simba market in Kigali, Rwanda's capital. It was one of her few possessions. She relished the afternoon ritual of brewing the rich coffee herself: mix the hot water and ground coffee in the glass cylinder, slowly depress the metal plunger to filter out the grounds, and pour. She allowed herself two butter cookies, and got to work on her computer at the dining room table.

Chapter 12) Something's Not Quite Right

A week later, Peter and Alicia were taking notes as the chimpanzees fed on the nectary, red flowers growing in a grove of tall *Symphonia* trees. The observers were lying on their backs in a patch of sunlight with their heads propped on their backpacks to reduce the strain on their necks of peering high into the tree canopy for hours. Ja was also lying on his back in the sun, fast asleep.

Ja, awakening, sensed something. "There are eyes," he said to Peter and Alicia. "Strange eyes."

"3 p.m. That's it for me for today," said Alicia, not picking up on Ja's uneasiness. "I'm heading back."

She asked Peter and Ja to track Chicken, who was the next day's follow, to his night nest.

Alicia noticed the dirty, battered, blue Japanese-made pick-up that was parked across the street from the field station at Mama Bernard's small inn in Kinihira. Mama Bernard was struggling to start a business. She offered Fanta, tea, coffee, beer and homemade cake to the many truck drivers who passed through the tiny village. Mama Bernard was betting on the future. Most of the drivers now just passed through Kinihira without stopping, eager to reach the larger town that was 30 miles further up the road. Few of the townsfolk had the cash to buy a drink. Alicia was rooting for Mama Bernard's success, and thus was pleased to see a truck in front of the inn.

Ja and Peter watched Chicken make his night nest, 40 feet up in a tree. Apple and Bee, Squash and Potato, and Rain nested nearby. Peter took the GPS coordinates of the nesting site, although he knew the place on his mental map.

"See you in the morning," Peter said, as the sun began to set. Ja headed back to his hut on the eastern edge of the reserve, and Peter to his family's clay house on the western side, near Kinihira. Neither said anything more about the "strange eyes," but neither would sleep well.

The two hunters squatted on the ridgeline and looked across the valley to the next hillside. "They're done work but we have to wait until midnight," said the older man.

"Why did we have to get here so soon?" asked the other.

"So we could see where they slept. How else could we find them in the dark?"

"Did you see where the babies are sleeping?"

Chapter 13) Kidnap

The full moon cast the forest in a warm glow. The men crept down the hillside, crossed the stream, and walked silently up the hill on the other side. Hunters, they were comfortable walking in the forest at night.

"I can see the nests," said the younger man.

"One of the mothers is right there," whispered the older, pointing upward.

He shouldered the shotgun and fired an unaimed blast. Then, he immediately swung the gun upward at the nests.

Chicken, Squash, carrying Potato, and Rain headed up, toward the canopy, shrieking in fear. Apple hesitated, stood on all fours, and looked over the edge of her nest. The second blast shattered her face. She fell to the moon-dappled ground. Bee, still asleep on Apple's belly, fell with her. Apple landed on her back, her arm still wrapped reflexively around her baby.

The men fell quickly on Bee, throwing a thick-stranded fishing net over her body, prying her off Apple, and wrapping her up in the net.

"Let's get out of here."

"Let's take the big one's body too. We can sell the meat."

"Too heavy to carry now. The money is with the baby."

"Let's just take her hands then."

Both Ja and Peter, sleeping fitfully because of Ja's premonition, heard the shots and screams from their from their homes at the edge of the forest. They now knew there were hunters in the reserve.

Alicia slept through the shots but did hear the pick-up start across the street in the middle of the night. She assumed that the driver had slept off Mama Bernard's beer and was resuming his journey. She fell back to sleep.

Chapter 14) The Payoff

The trip down-mountain to Gisenyi took only 90 minutes but seemed endless to Bee. She was trussed in the back of the truck, alone, being tossed and thrown as it lurched over ruts and potholes. Most people were asleep, and the truck passed heard but not seen through the small villages that straddled the road.

The square in front of the bus station was likewise deserted but the truck pulled around to the back of Madam Chen's store to assure privacy. The men had called her from the road. She was waiting in the doorway.

Bee fought but was no match for the men as they unwrapped her, threw her into a heavy wooden cage, and snapped a lock on the cage door. It was only then that she realized that she had been wrapped up with Apple's hands, which had fallen to the floor. A few of the poachers' shotgun pellets had penetrated Bee's hand. She cried out in pain and fear.

There was another box beside hers, and an unseen beast stirred and yowled from within.

Bee could barely stand or turn around in her box. She could look out through a crack, but it was dark and she only could see only a woman giving two men some paper.

"There's another baby up there," one of the men told Madam Chen.

"Let's get rid of this one first," she answered.

There was a dirty towel on the bottom of Bee's cage. She scrunched it up and held it to her stomach as she sat, knees-to-chest. She began to rock methodically back and forth, crying, without tears, for her lost world.

The men left. Madam Chen turned out the lights and went upstairs to her apartment. Bee rocked and cried. The beast beside her paced in tight, relentless circles.

Chapter 15) Chained

Enough light passed through a high window in the back room to allow Bee to know it was dawn. The woman padded silently down the stairs in her tattered running shoes and disappeared into the store in front. Bee could hear cars, trucks and buses, with which she was familiar because at Gishwati the road ran right along one edge of the small forest. She could hear people's voices, seemingly far away. People's voices were also familiar. Bee heard and saw people at Gishwati as they walked along the road, gathering firewood, fetching water, going to school, tending goats, and visiting relatives and friends. But this was different. She could not watch and listen from the trees above, secure in the arms of her mother. She was alone, except for whatever was living in the crate beside hers, and she was hungry and in pain.

Madam Chen came in to the back room and squeezed a rotten apple through the slats of Bee's cage. The apple turned to mush and dripped down the sides, forming a puddle on the bottom. Bee licked up every drop. Chen shoved something else into the cage next to Bee's. Bee could hear some quiet snuffling.

Chen suddenly stuck a stout stick through the slats behind Bee's head and pulled her roughly to the front of the cage. She pinned Bee's head against the small opening, looped a length of heavy chain around the back of Bee's neck, and snapped the chain shut with a padlock under Bee's chin. Bee could barely breathe or swallow. Madam Chen removed the stick. Bee fingered the heavy chain and tried to slip it over her head. She couldn't.

Madam Chen went back into her store.

Chapter 16) Finding Apple

Ja could not sleep and had gone to the forest while it was still dark. Peter had rushed to the field station before dawn and awakened Alicia, telling her about the gunshots. They had skipped breakfast and rushed to the nest site, fearing that something bad had happened. Ja was waiting on the trail. He pressed two shotgun casings into Peter's hand.

"Apple and Bee," he said.

"Oh God."

"Very bad," said Ja.

He led them to Apple's handless and nearly headless body.

"Where's Bee?"

"Don't know. I looked everywhere."

Alicia knelt over Apple's body, tears rolling silently down her cheeks.

"Who could have done this?" she asked nobody in particular.

"Nobody local," said Peter. "These are high-end shotgun shells. None of our farmers even owns a shotgun."

"But they're mad because of the baby-shaking," she said.

"Dr. Alicia, they may be angry but you know they would not go this far."

She told Peter to send Ja to bring six men. She and Peter then used their machetes to cut some saplings and vines to make a crude stretcher. They lifted Apple's body onto the stretcher, and Alicia covered her with her jacket.

Alicia and Peter sat down to wait for the men. Peter pointed upward. Stone, Chicken, Squash, holding Potato extra tightly, Rain, and Carrot sat motionlessly above, in complete silence.

"Let's back off," said Alicia. The two moved upslope.

Stone came down first, uncharacteristically hesitant and

silent.

He walked to the stretcher and touched Apple's foot cautiously with the back of an outstretched hand. He smelled his fingers, and took a step closer. He picked up a corner of Alicia's jacket and peered at Apple's mutilated body. He smelled her stomach, as if he were looking for his beloved Bee.

The others came down and joined him, and soon there were nineteen chimpanzees gathered reverentially around the body. Some groomed one another, some scratched their own sides, shoulders, and armpits nervously, and some embraced and whimpered softly.

After 30 minutes, the voices of the approaching men broke the silence. The death of an animal at the hands of a hunter was not shocking to these Batwa men. They knew Ja was upset, but continued to gossip until Peter instructed them in Kinyarwanda to pick up the stretcher and carry Apple's body out to the road.

The forest exploded with screams and shrieks. Chimpanzees ran and seemingly flew, ripping up saplings and breaking off branches that they threw at the people below. A storm of urine and feces fell to the ground. Alicia felt fear for the first time in her life with the chimpanzees.

"Just walk," said Peter steadily. "They're upset but they won't hurt us. They *know* that we didn't do this. They saw it."

"Shouldn't we bury her?" asked Peter after a while.

"We'll take her to Ruhengiri so the Gorilla Doctors can do an autopsy."

A crowd of curious and bewildered human onlookers surrounded the bearers as they emerged from the forest at the edge of the road. The chimpanzees watched from above. The men slid Apple's body into the rear of Alicia's old Land Rover.

Alicia called Ramona, the head vet at Gorilla Doctors, and asked if she could send over a dead chimpanzee.

Gorilla Doctors have been providing medical care to wild and orphaned mountain gorillas in the Virunga mountains of Rwanda for four decades. Without their work, and the conservation and research efforts of the Dian Fossey Fund, the mountain gorillas would have been driven to extinction long ago. Most of the veterinarians' work, like removing a poacher's snare from a gorilla's wrist, is done on the steep, forested mountainsides of the Volcanoes National Park. But the doctors also have a field station in the bustling city of Ruhengiri, at the base of mountains. The station has a well-equipped clinical laboratory and an operating room to conduct surgeries on gorillas. The room was also used to conduct *post mortem* examinations on dead gorillas.

At the start of Alicia's study, the Gorilla Doctors had told her that they would treat ill or injured chimpanzees at Gishwati and perform autopsies when the need arose.

"There's no doubt about the cause of death... gunshot," Alicia told Ramona, "but we might as well learn everything we can from her body."

"How old?" asked Dr. Ramona.

"About 22, lactating."

"Where's the baby?"

"We don't know."

"Probably stolen," said Ramona. "We'll alert our contacts to be on the lookout for a baby chimp. You coming along?"

"No, I'm sending Peter. I have to contact the police. And Peter will have to come back up here to help me."

"OK, let's stay in close touch."

Ruhengiri was only 40 miles away from Gishwati as the crow flies, but it was three hours away by road.

"Turn right around and come back, OK?" Alicia told Peter. "We've got lots to do here."

Alicia called the district police headquarters as Peter drove off. "We've had a chimpanzee murdered and her baby kidnapped," she reported, after finally finding someone who could speak English.

"We'll come over," said the police lieutenant on the other end.

The district police station was a two-hour drive away. Alicia waved to Ja to follow her, and they returned to the forest.

They could not find, or even hear, any chimpanzees. The apes had simply vanished.

"They are afraid," said Ja.

After two more hours of searching, Alicia said: "I have to meet the police. Can you keep looking?"

"I will stay all night," said Ja.

Oh God! Alicia thought. *The hunters might come back?*

Chapter 17) Lieutenant Habimana

Lieutenant Martin Habimana was tall, slender, clean-shaven and stately. He had served with distinction in the Rwandan army, and had taken a position in the Rutsiro District branch of the Rwandan National Police when he left the military. He spoke English, French and Kinyarwanda, and had taken courses in forensics and investigative policing in South Africa. He unfolded himself unhurriedly from the passenger seat of the small police sedan, and met Alicia at the gate of the field station.

"Hello. I called you. Dr. Alicia Oliveira." She extended her hand.

"Nice to meet you. Lieutenant Martin Habimana." He shook her hand. Each noted that the other wore no rings.

"As I told you on the phone..." began Alicia, but the lieutenant interrupted.

"We'll get to that," he said. "But first, tell me about you and what you are doing here? You don't seem to be Rwandan. Let's start with your passport."

Alicia rolled her eyes but went to her room and retrieved her passport from the small metal box she kept under her bed. She went back out to the field station parking area and handed Habimana her passport.

"Brazilian? Why are you in Rwanda?"

"I wanted to study chimpanzees, and we don't have any in Brazil."

"Really? Nowhere in South America?"

"We have monkeys but no apes."

"But there are chimpanzees everywhere in Africa. Why Rwanda?"

"Because these chimpanzees live in a tiny forest, and I'm interested in finding out how they get enough to eat." That was not the whole truth but it was enough for now.

"You could be asking that question about all of the *people* who live up here," he said. "Who pays you?"

Alicia did not like the drift of this conversation. The

lieutenant was putting her on the defensive.

"I have a grant from the Ark Foundation. It pays me a stipend of twelve thousand dollars a year, provides rent for the field station, an old truck, and salaries for a cook and a few field assistants, which, by the way, help to feed people up here."

"Twelve thousand is a lot in Rwanda." It was indeed twice the lieutenant's annual salary.

"I have to pay my own airfare, and buy my own health insurance and food. I also paid to fix this place up."

"There's only a tourist visa in this passport. Do you have a research visa?"

"I applied for it. I have to pick it up when I go to Kigali."

Now he had her. He could now legally prevent her from re-entering the forest and could even end the study because she had technically been conducting research without a research visa.

What does this guy want? thought Alicia. "Would you like come inside and have some coffee?" she asked, falling back reflexively to the custom of her native Brazil to serve coffee during any meaningful discussion.

She summoned Leonard, who hastily built up the fire, boiled water, and brought the ground coffee and hot water to the dining room table so Alicia could do her magic with the French press.

"Milk, sugar?" she asked, handing him a steaming mug.

"Both please, thank you. Now, tell me what happened this morning."

"Peter and Ja heard gunshots around 1 a.m."

"Who's Peter and Ja?"

She filled him in on her assistants.

"You hired a Batwa? That's a joke."

"He's not always on time but he sure knows the forest and knows how to build trails."

"How do you know that he didn't fire the shots? Batwa are hunters, you know."

The thought had never crossed Alicia's mind.

"I'm sure it's not him. He really cares about the chimpanzees. He's in the forest now, watching to see that none of the others gets shot."

"Oh really," said the lieutenant, suspiciously. "OK, so what happened after they *heard* the shots?"

"Ja was the first to find the body of the dead chimpanzee."

"Oh really." The lieutenant was taking notes in a small lined notebook now.

"Peter and I arrived just after dawn."

"Why did you arrive together?

Alicia flared red at the unasked question. "Peter sleeps in his family's house in the village. We meet here every morning and go into the forest together."

"What did you find?"

"The chimpanzee's name was Apple."

"Who gave it the name?"

"Peter. As I told you, he's been watching and protecting these chimpanzees for years."

"Who pays him?"

"Nobody, until I hired him as my assistant last year."

"Do the chimpanzees have their own names, that they call each other?"

"We don't know."

"How old was Apple?"

"We think about 22. And she had a 19-month-old baby."

"So Apple was dead?"

"Head blown off with a shotgun."

"How do you know it was a shotgun?"

"Here." Alicia handed the lieutenant the shell casings.

"And her hands were hacked off and taken."

The lieutenant grimaced. He knew that this used to happen a lot. Tourists actually used to buy dried ape hands to use as ashtrays. But gorillas and chimpanzees had been effectively protected in Rwanda for 20 years.

"Where's the baby?"

"Missing."

"Did you look for it?"

"Yes, and Ja still is," answered Alicia, immediately regretting her words.

"Boy or girl?"

"Girl. Her name is Bee."

"Nursing?"

"Yes, but she was also starting to eat solid foods."

"Any distinguishing marks?"

"Bee has a black L-shaped spot on her right cheek. Her face and ears are still pink so you can see the spot."

"Any strangers been around, in the forest or in the village?"

"We had the feeling yesterday that there was somebody watching us in the forest, but we didn't see anybody." She didn't say that it was Ja who had had the feeling, and that she had ignored him.

"How about the village?"

"Not that I know of. Mama Bernard would be the best one to answer that."

"Who's Mama Bernard?"

"She runs a small inn across... "

Alicia suddenly remembered: "I saw an old truck in front of the inn yesterday. Old and beat up, blue, Japanese-made I think. Never saw it up here before."

"Who was driving it?"

"Don't know. Let's ask Mama Bernard."

They walked across the unpaved street to the inn, which was little more than the converted living room of a small house. A 12-year-old boy, still in his neat brown school uniform, pored over his homework, sitting on one of the four chairs that ringed the only table in the room. A glassless window opened to the street, allowing some late afternoon light to fall on the boy's schoolwork. A Primus beer poster hung over a wooden bench that ran along one wall.

Mama Bernard was nearly as tall as the lieutenant, and just as stately. But she was nervous because she had not yet got a license for the inn.

"Yes, there were two men here yesterday afternoon. They were dirty and rough. They had a Primus and hard-boiled eggs, and then left."

"Where did they go?" Mama and the lieutenant spoke quietly but their voices reverberated off the room's concrete walls and floor. A few passersby stared through the window and eavesdropped.

"I don't know. Their truck was still here when we went to bed. They didn't drive away until the middle of the night. I don't know where they were all that time."

"Did you know them?" Mama Bernard thought she heard a note of suspicion.

"One was older and the other was in his 20s. I think the young one used to live around here but I haven't seen or heard of him for a few years."

"Where does he live now?"

"I don't know."

"Did you see the license plates on the truck?"

"No."

"Rwandan... Gisenyi," said the boy.

"I want to talk to this Ja," the lieutenant said to Alicia as they returned to his waiting car. "And to Peter."

"Now?"

"Tomorrow. It's 4 o'clock and I have to get back to the office."

"A chimpanzee has been murdered and her baby kidnapped, and you're going back to the office?" Alicia exploded in frustration.

"Dr. Oliveira, in all respect, only people are murdered or kidnapped," the lieutenant said icily. "Rwanda owns these chimpanzees. They're animals and they're our property, and somebody has killed one and stolen another. Animals are killed and stolen all the time up here."

They exchanged cell phone numbers. He refolded himself into the car, and the driver sped off.

Chapter 18) Ja Under Suspicion

The two police sedans sped up to the cluster of abandoned, roofless Batwa houses. Lieutenant Habimana got out of one and four armed uniformed officers got out of the other. Three Batwa women were talking idly and cutting up some small branches for firewood while their children were waking up and coming out of the small huts that were arrayed around the empty houses.

"Lieutenant Habimana, district police. We want to talk to Ja."

The women exchanged glances. The children, sleep still in their eyes, peered out from behind their mothers' skirts.

"He didn't come home last night."

"Are you his wife?"

"Yes."

"Which one is your house?"

She pointed toward a hut with her machete.

"Do you mind putting your machete down?"

The hut was made of limbs and leaves, but was sturdy and dry. A piece of cloth hung over the open doorway.

The lieutenant nodded to the officers. They pulled back the curtain and began to toss the house.

They found a smoldering cooking fire, a mattock, a rusty shovel, a hammer that was missing one claw, a 20-liter plastic jerry can with fermenting banana beer, a 10-liter jerry can with some water, a clay pot of dried beans, some bunched ears of corn, six chicken eggs, four blankets, some assorted clothing and battered housewares, a brand new pair of rubber boots, and an unworn men's green shirt and matching pants. No Ja, no shotgun, no shells, not even a spear or a snare.

Habimana signaled to the men to search the other huts. They did not find Ja or, except for a few snares in one hut, anything else of interest.

"Contact me when Ja comes back."

"How would we do that?" said Ja's wife. Nobody in this enclave had a cellphone yet.

"Go back to headquarters," the lieutenant told the four officers. "We'll drive around to the field station."

Chapter 19) Bee Makes A Friend

Bee's morning was not going well either. Madam Chen dumped the leftovers of a bowl of salty noodle soup into her cage. Bee licked it up eagerly, but the salt worsened her increasing dehydration.

Chen swung the body of a dead rat into the other cage. The rat had been run over by a bus in the square and spent its last broken minutes dying behind a bag of charcoal in front of the store. The occupant of the cage sounded grateful for the rat.

"God, it stinks in here," said Chen. She would have to get

somebody to clean the crates until she was able to complete the arrangements to ship their occupants to China.

Apple had taught Bee not to pee or poop in the nest. Like all apes, Bee would do her business first thing in the morning when she left the nest, and the mess would fall to the forest floor. Tree dwellers never contact their urine or feces, greatly reducing the chance of reinfection by any parasites that they might have picked up.

But tree dwellers locked in cages can't escape it, and Bee had had to go in her cage. She made her little piles and puddles in one corner, and covered them with the dirty towel. But this left her without the towel to clutch in her loneliness, and it all added to her misery.

Chen returned a few hours later with a man.

"I'll drop the chain into the cage. You open the door and I'll grab the chain," she said.

Bee made a beeline out of the cage, but she reached the end of the chain after five feet and was jerked backward. Madam Chen held the other end, and was locking it to a post. Bee thought about attacking her but decided to stay as far away as possible.

"OK, let's do the other one."

A rope protruded from that cage. Chen slid the rope into the cage, while the man opened the door just a crack. She passed the rope to her other hand through the crack. There was an explosive yowl, and Chen screamed in pain.

Holding the rope with her now-bleeding hand, Chen pulled the animal out roughly and kicked it away from her.

"Damn you," she said to the cat, which was now flicking its dark eyes from Chen to the man to the ape. It too decided to retreat to the end of the rope, which was attached with a slipknot around his slender neck.

Chen tied the rope to the same post that held Bee's chain.

"Take these stinking crates into the back alley and scrub them out," she told the man. The rat tail slid to the floor. "And wash this floor too."

The man lugged the crates out to the alley. Chen went into the store to tend to her bleeding hand.

Ape and cat stared at each other, ten feet apart, each at the end of a five-foot tether.

Bee had seen this type of cat, a serval, in the Gishwati Forest, but she had been up in a tree and the cats were always on the ground. Three times the size of a house cat, the serval's lithe frame stood on disproportionately long legs. It had long rounded ears and a glorious gold coat with constellations of dark lines and spots.

Minutes went by. The man returned and began to scrub the floor. Both animals took the opportunity to lick water from the floor when he rinsed it. They circled away from the man as he worked, as if the three were choreographed.

Both animals thought separately about attacking the man. The serval decided not to attack because the man was so much bigger. Servals were predators but they killed only small animals, like squirrels, mice, and birds. Bee realized that an attack would do no good. Even if she did drive him off, she would still be chained.

The man slid the crates back into place, and went to the front of the store. He returned minutes later with Madam Chen.

"No need to lock 'em up in the cages," she said. "It's too hard to get 'em out. They're not going anywhere."

"Fill that with water." She gave the man an old rusted can that had once held British-made tea biscuits. "Gotta keep 'em alive until I can ship 'em."

The man and woman left through the door to the store. The ape and cat went back to staring.

Bee had no idea that she would be sold to a wealthy Chinese person and kept chained as a pet in a house if she was lucky, or as an attraction in a store or bar if she was not.

The serval had no idea that he would be sold to a Chinese merchant and slaughtered. His luxurious coat would be sold as a fashion accessory, and his organs would be sold to superstitious customers as cures for various illnesses and ailments.

The serval was hungry and confused by being tied up. He hurt from a wound where the snare that had captured him had dug into his front leg. He was just a juvenile, and he missed his mother and littermates.

Bee was also hungry and confused. She hurt from the gunshot wound in her hand, and desperately missed the affection and warmth of her mother and the companionship of her community.

The difference was that Bee could *think about* her misery, as well as feel it. Was her mother dead or captured? Was this woman her new mother? Where was she?

Neither the serval nor the ape would have attacked the other in their former life, but here, 10 feet apart, they were wary of one another.

The serval approached the can of water, which had been placed between them, next to the post. He drank heavily. In her forest life, Bee had gotten most of her fluids by nursing on her mother, and had only once put her lips and nose into a puddle. She watched the cat and felt the dryness in her mouth. She inched closer.

The cat finished drinking and lay down a foot from the can.

Bee stretched out her arm, stuck a hand into what remained of the water, and licked water from her little fist, watching the cat warily. She dipped and drank, until the can was empty.

She moved away a few feet, entering the cage that had been set there with its door open. At least she was protected in the cage from the sides, back, and top. The rag was there but was still too wet and dirty to provide any comfort. Bee leaned against the back of the cage and fell asleep.

Bee woke up suddenly when Madam Chen came into the back room.

"Well, well. Look at the two best friends."

Bee was startled to find the serval curled in her lap, now eyeing Chen warily.

Chen threw another rat to the serval, which leapt out of the cage, seized the rat, and began to tear it apart. Chen gave Bee nothing to eat.

"Nothing rotten enough yet for you," she said.

Bee had tasted meat after a hunt, but it had usually been thoroughly chewed and mashed up with leaves by Stone or another chimpanzee.

Bee fingered some rat guts, and licked the blood from her finger. Hunger is hunger. She ate a piece of liver and nibbled on a bit of leg.

Bee wondered if the cat had intentionally left some of the rat for her. She once again sat in the back of the cage, and the serval, having finished the rat, crept back into her lap. The serval was actually too big to be *in* Bee's lap. He was draped over Bee's lap, like a blanket, which suited Bee just fine. She leaned over the cat and embraced it. The two frightened animals fell asleep, indulging in each other's touch.

Chapter 20) The Investigation Continues

Lieutenant Habimana had called Alicia from the Batwa village and asked her and Peter to wait at the field station until he could get there. He arrived at 10 a.m. and found a cranky and impatient Alicia and an apprehensive Peter. There was no hospitable cup of coffee today.

"Well, you sure set off some alarms," he said to Alicia.

She knew what he meant. She had not wanted to play the H.E. card, and so far she had not.

"I checked on your research visa. It is ready, and had been given top priority by H.E.'s office. How did that happen?"

H.E., short for His Excellency, is the name that Rwandans use to refer to their charismatic president, Paul Kagame.

"Why is our president pulling strings for a Brazilian doctoral student?"

Alicia explained that President Kagame had led a farming and trade delegation to Brazil five years previously. The delegation visited the expansive and successful Red River Ranch to observe farming and ranching on the steep-sided hills of Brazil's Atlantic Coastal Rainforest. The ranch's wealthy and influential owner, Senhor Mauricio Carvalho, had hosted a sumptuous Brazilian-style barbecue lunch for the delegation at his ranch, and then invited his Rwandan guests to take a short walk to a banana grove to see "his" endangered golden lion tamarin monkeys.

"These monkeys occur only in this area and were almost extinct," Carvalho explained. "The Smithsonian bred them in zoos and reintroduced them here. They're thriving," he said proudly.

"But they are so small," teased H.E. "We have *big* apes, gorillas, and chimpanzees in Rwanda."

"I know," said Carvalho. "One of the students who works with the tamarins is in love with apes and wants desperately to study them."

"That is attainable," said H.E., handing his host the card of his chief-of-staff. "Call when the student is ready to come."

Alicia was that student. Carvalho had deemed it unnecessary to tell H.E. that he was in love with her and had proposed to her. She had declined, preferring instead to go to university and then to graduate school with the goal of studying apes in Africa. When she had gotten to the point of designing her doctoral thesis, Carvalho had made the call and doors had opened.

"So that's the story," said Alicia, after the long explanation to Habimana. She left out the love and marriage angle.

"I'd like to look through your field station, just to be

thorough."

Alicia again rolled her eyes. This time Habimana noticed her frustration.

"Would you prefer that I discontinue the investigation?"

"No, of course not."

"I have alerted the army to be on the lookout for a baby ape at their road checkpoints and border patrols, and we informed customs officials at border crossings, especially in Goma."

"Thank you."

The lieutenant was opening drawers and checking closets. He peered up into the open roof trusses, and into the outside latrine and shower stall.

"I'd like to speak with Peter now."

The conversation with Peter yielded no surprises. His story was consistent with Alicia's and Mama Bernard's. When the lieutenant asked about the strangers in the blue truck, Peter said that he did remember a young man from a nearby village who had stolen money from his own mother that she had earned by working long hours picking tea for the equivalent of one dollar a day. The man had left in disgrace. Peter did not know where he was now.

"I'd like to speak with Ja now."

"We'll never find him. He's scared of the police and will evaporate in the forest. Not guilt, just fear."

Peter actually had a good idea about where Ja could be found in the forest, but he did not share it with Habimana or Alicia.

"I think he's involved," said Habimana. "He may not have done this himself but he may have been working with the two strange guys."

"No way," said Peter.

"Stay in touch," said the lieutenant. "We also have the Gisenyi police looking for a blue pick-up."

Chapter 21) Camera Trap

Habimana gone, Alicia began to think about work. It was too late to do a follow. They would collect the camera traps and log in the pictures.

The camera traps! she thought.

"Peter, why didn't we think about the camera traps? We'll have some pictures of the poachers if they used the trails."

"We don't think that Ja was involved, but suppose that we see that he was?" asked Peter.

"If it was him, we'll turn him in. But he knows where the traps are and would not allow himself to be photographed."

Camera traps are weatherproof, battery-powered cameras that field observers attach to trees at waist level next to trails in the forest. Any movement in front of the camera causes it to take a picture. The cameras take color photos during the day, and at night they take black-and-white pictures with an infrared flash. All of the photos are automatically stamped with date and time. The traps provide records of chimpanzee movements when the observers are not present, and they also catch images of other mammals and birds. The team first discovered that servals lived in Gishwati when they appeared in the photos.

"Let's get all eight of them," said Alicia. "We'll start by looking at pictures from the ones on the trails that lead from Apple's nest to the road."

Alicia and Peter split up, although they had walkie-talkies to stay in touch. They brought the traps back to the field station. Reviewing the trap photos was usually an exciting and pleasant Friday afternoon task. The team never knew what they would find. But today, it was all business.

They removed the memory card from the trap that had been nearest to Apple's nest, and inserted it into Alicia's computer. The photos downloaded so rapidly that Peter and Alicia could barely glimpse the images until the download was complete.

"Let's not erase the card this time," said Alicia. "It might be evidence."

The trap took a photo when the camera's sensor was

triggered by motion. There were always plenty of pictures of "nothing" that were taken when birds flew past the camera and were gone by the time the picture was taken. Even a blowing leaf or heavy rain would activate the shutter. Once a photo was taken, the camera was set to wait for 60 seconds before it took another picture. This saved battery power and disc space by not taking 60 photos a minute of the same animal walking past the camera. But there were still hundreds of photos to review.

"There," blurted Alicia.

The trap had recorded a black-and-white image of one arm and the hip of a person walking along the side of the path.

"Looks like a man. It's not one of us," said Peter, "and it's probably not a Batwa. Too tall, and the pants are in pretty good shape."

The time stamp read "10:20 PM, 8 October 2014".

"That's the night that Apple was murdered!" said Peter. "So we know there was a stranger in the forest that night."

"We knew that already," said Alicia. "Oh, and by the way, Lieutenant Habimana says that only people can be murdered, not chimps."

"Oh," said Peter, storing this idea for later thought. They finished looking at the images but the only other photo of interest was of a small group of side-striped jackals.

"Whoever the stranger was, he must have stayed off the trails and walked through the underbrush. Is that a machete in his hand?"

"Can't be sure," said Peter.

"Let's look at the card from camera that was on the path near the road," said Alicia.

This camera had been set up inside the forest, 300 feet from the road on a path favored by locals to walk between the western and eastern edges of the forest. It faced the road, to catch the faces of the trespassers as they entered.

Alicia and Peter saw seven days of pictures of themselves entering and leaving the forest, and a few of some villagers passing through. One carried a machete and branches, but they did not stop to try to identify her. Finally, on the last day, they got what they wanted, almost.

"There's two!" said Peter. "1:30 a.m., 9 October 2014"

"They're carrying something between them."

"And a gun."

"And machetes."

"One looks like the same guy in the other photo."

They hurried to match up the height and clothing of the men in this picture with that of the man in the other that was taken earlier on the same night.

"It's him."

"That's probably Bee in some sort of sling."

"But we can only see their backs, not their faces."

"Get Mama Bernard," said Alicia. "Maybe she can identify the clothing. I'll call Habimana."

Mama Bernard stared at the computer in Alicia's small office: "I think that's them."

Habimana asked Alicia to send him the photos by e-mail. He called back after a few minutes.

"OK, we know that there were two strangers involved, both African, and that they are probably driving a blue pick-up that is registered in Gisenyi," he said. "Ja's not in the pictures but we still can't rule him out. And oh, by the way, good work. Maybe you should be a cop."

"What now?" Alicia asked him.

"Ordinarily, I'd drop it. Just another poaching. But chimpanzees are endangered, and given your connection with H.E.… "

"You don't really think I would just call him?"

"He'll hear about it soon enough. He has eyes and ears

everywhere. When he finds out, he'll ask what is being done. I'll want to have an answer."

Chapter 22) Peter Reaches Out

Alicia asked Peter to spend the rest of the day reviewing and filing the camera trap photos of interest, cross-referenced by day, time, camera location and subject. He purged the cards, except for the two pictures of the poachers, changed the batteries, and prepared the cameras to reinstall the next day.

It was boring work, and he had time to think. There were several good shots of Bee riding on Apple's back, and many of the other chimpanzees as well. The chimpanzees sometimes approached the camera closely and examined it. In one sequence, Chicken seemed to be observing his reflection in the small glass lens. Peter had seen the chimpanzees study themselves in the lens of the camera that he often carried to get shots that could be used to identify all of the chimpanzees that he kept in a "mug book."

Scientists elsewhere had found that lab chimpanzees would groom themselves in a mirror or open their mouths and examine their tongue and teeth. This meant that a chimpanzee knew that the image in the mirror was *itself*. Once they formed this self-concept, they never slapped at the image in the mirror or looked behind the mirror for another ape. The scientists concluded that chimpanzees had "self-awareness". They knew the difference between themselves and other chimpanzees.

Peter was not aware of all of this lab research but he had

reached the same conclusion over the years. He knew that they knew themselves and each of the other chimps in the Gishwati group. Stone never tickled Potato behind the knees.

This gave Peter an idea. The events of the day had given him reason to think that they would catch Apple's murderer and recover Bee. If only he could reassure Stone.

He quickly went to the "Bee" photo file and found the best facial close-up, which clearly showed her big pink ears and her pink face with the black L-shaped spot on her right cheek.

Then he did the same for Stone. He arranged the two photos on one landscape page, with Bee on the right looking at Stone, on the left. Stone seemed to be staring back at Bee.

Would Stone understand? Would Peter be able to assure him that they were looking for Bee and would return her to the group?

He printed the page, and put it in his pack.

"I didn't finish all of the filing, but the cameras are ready to go tomorrow," Peter told Alicia. "Rain's our follow tomorrow. I'm going to try to find where she'll nest tonight so we can find her in the morning. Then I'll head home."

"Goodnight, Peter. Thanks for all the good work today."

Peter was actually looking for Stone. He got lucky and found

Stone and Rain. Both were near the road. He sat below as they made their night nests, listening to the explosive popping and cracking of the branches that would become the skeletons of the apes' nests. He pulled the printed page out of his pack and held it up for Stone to see. He then covered the print with some dry leaves, and left.

Chapter 23) Stone Gets the Message

"Good morning, Peter," Alicia said as he joined her in the dining room the next morning, just as Leonard set down her oatmeal.

"I found Rain's nest."

"You'll have to follow her by yourself. Maybe Ja will show up."

"Are you OK?" Peter asked. Leonard brought his steaming igikoma.

"Yes, but I've got to meet some tourists who are coming today to see the chimps."

"Big group?"

"Just two, both young women who saw gorillas yesterday and want to see chimps today. One of the girl's mothers is the CEO of Gaslight International, the company that's trying to make electricity from the methane under Lake Kivu. Big bucks."

"Coming up from Ruhengiri?"

"Yes, they should be here by 10. I'll radio you and we'll meet you and Rain."

"Rain was with Stone last night, and some of the others were nearby. Should be an easy walk. They've been staying near the road since Bee disappeared," Peter reported. "Do you want me to follow her or put out the cameras?"

"Let's do the follow. We can put out the cameras this afternoon," Alicia decided.

Peter finished his breakfast, grabbed the lunches that Leonard had packed for him and Ja, and headed for the forest. He went straight to Rain's and Stone's nests of last night, but when he got there he was looking down for the little pile of leaves rather than up at the nests.

"He took it," said Ja from behind, startling Peter.

"God, you scared me. Where have you been?" asked Peter.

"Here, guarding the chimps," Ja answered.

"The police are looking for you," said Peter.

"I know, but I don't have time for police now."

"We have a picture from the camera traps of the two men that stole Bee, but the police still think that you might have been involved."

"What do you and Dr. Alicia think?"

"No way."

"But I am a Batwa hunter," said Ja, with trace of a wry smile.

"We might be able to catch these guys and get Bee back," said Peter.

"Stone looked at the paper for a long time," Ja reported.

"Dr. Alicia doesn't know I left it here."

"You and I know some other important things that she does not."

"At least not yet," said Peter. "Which way did Rain and Stone go?"

"There," pointed Ja, "but we won't be able to find them."

"Do you think Stone understood what I was trying to say?" asked Peter.

"I understood, and I can't read," said Ja.

Chapter 24) Adventure Tourism

Trekking chimpanzees and birds at Gishwati had been advertised as "soft adventure tourism." That meant moderately difficult walking up and down hills in the forest, crossing creeks on fallen logs, passing below the magnificent Kazaneza Falls by stepping on slick stones in the rushing river, and foregoing bathrooms with running water. An encounter with a bush viper or a swarm of bees or cold, rainy weather was always possible.

The shiny black Toyota Land Cruiser pulled through the open gate of the field station a few minutes after 10 a.m. The car was freshly washed except for some mud splotches and dust that had accumulated on this morning's drive up the mountain.

Augustin leapt from the driver's seat with a beaming smile. He was wearing smartly pressed khaki pants, an ironed safari shirt, and almost-new L.L. Bean hiking boots. The boots had been given to him by a previous client who had worn them for only one day of gorilla trekking.

"Good morning, Dr. Alicia," Augustin said in almost unaccented English. He was clean-shaven and smelled lightly of cologne.

"Good morning. Augustin. How's business at Rwanda Eco-Treks?"

"Too busy, but we'll slow down when the rains come next month."

"I think they're here already," said Alicia.

Two young women, in their early 20s, got out of the back seat of the Toyota.

Alicia approached them, hand extended. "Hi, I'm Alicia Oliveira. Welcome to Gishwati. I study the chimpanzees here."

"Hi, I'm Elizabeth Weatherby and this is my friend, Whitney Logan."

"What brings you to Rwanda?"

"My mom's company is trying to make enough electricity to supply all of western Rwanda. We're on summer vacation, and she asked us to visit her for a few weeks," said Elizabeth.

"How do you like it?"

"Amazing. The history, the genocide, the hills, the animals – we saw gorillas yesterday."

"The tea plantations that we passed on the way up here are so beautiful," said Whitney.

The girls were dressed in the newest REI field outfits and boots. They had obviously changed since yesterday's gorilla trek because their clothes were spotless this morning. Elizabeth wore a multi-pocketed vest that bulged with her supplies for the trek. Whitney wore a fashionable backpack and had an expensive Nikon slung around her neck.

"What gorilla group did you see?" asked Alicia.

"Group 13 – 32 gorillas. A beautiful silverback, and the babies were incredible. We watched them for an hour."

"Well, I'm afraid you won't see many chimpanzees today, and not from very close. We had some poaching last week, and the chimpanzees are scared now."

"But they're endangered," said Whitney. "How can there be poaching?"

"We have no guards at Gishwati. Just me and my field assistants," said Alicia.

After a short pause, Alicia changed the subject: "OK, let's get going. Anybody need to use the bathroom? Better to go now. The latrine is right over there."

The women returned, drying their hands on their pants.

"Do you have water to drink?" Alicia asked.

"We each have two bottles, and some power bars," answered Whitney.

"You coming?" Alicia asked Augustin.

"No, I'll stay with the car today." Alicia knew that Augustin always stayed with the car. He did have to watch over it, even though the chance of mischief was minimal within the fence around the field station. Augustin didn't like to sweat or get dirty.

"Call me if you need anything," said Augustin, waving his smart phone to the girls as they followed Alicia out of the gate.

Alicia called Peter on the walkie-talkie as they walked to the entrance of the forest: "We're on our way. Where are you?"

"On the ridgeline trail near the falls. No sign of the chimps. You can show them the nests from last night on the way in, about 500 feet down the trail on your right."

Chapter 25) Snake

The three women walked briskly down the first steep hillside and up the next. Alicia pointed out Stone's and Rain's nests from the previous night and explained the chimpanzees' nesting habits. Whitney took a telephoto lens from her backpack and took pictures of the structures.

"She's a journalism major," Elizabeth told Alicia as Whitney snapped away.

"You both seem to be in pretty good shape," said Alicia.

"I swim and run cross-country for our college teams," said Elizabeth.

"And I'm on the starting soccer... uh, football team," added Whitney, stowing the long lens.

"She's actually an All-American, defense," said Elizabeth.

"You should both have an easy day then," said Alicia. "Ready to move on?"

They had to walk over the Gumba River on the slippery log.

"Let me take your pack and camera, just in case," Alicia offered.

"It's OK, thanks," said Whitney.

Alicia crossed effortlessly. The other two women did some arm-waving to keep their balance.

"Yoga helps," said Elizabeth.

They trudged up the steep hillside, stopping once for a drink of water.

"Peter's just ahead," said Alicia.

Peter impressed the women with his welcoming smile and sparkling white teeth.

"Peter, meet Elizabeth and Whitney," said Alicia.

All three said: "Hi." Peter wondered which of the young women had the rich mother.

"No chimps. Not a knuckle print, a footprint, or a peep. They have not been in the bamboo grove this morning. Ja doesn't even know where they are," Peter said, nodding to the gnarled and disheveled man who stood a few feet away.

"This is Ja -" began Alicia, but she was interrupted by an explosion of shrieks.

"Wow, there they are," said Peter, "on the other side of the

Pfunda."

"Is it a hunt?" asked Alicia.

"Not hunt," said Ja. "They are scared."

"Oh, God," said Alicia. "Let's go. Can you girls keep up?"

They walked rapidly, sometimes on a trail and sometimes taking shortcuts through the forest. Ja led the way, but it was tough going through the underbrush.

They reached Kazaneza Falls, and stopped to catch their breath. Whitney began to take pictures.

"We'll stop on the way back," said Alicia. "I want to see what the chimps are up to."

She pointed with her head to the top of the next ridge. The chimpanzees had stopped shrieking, but some soft whining could still be heard.

Ja and Peter exchanged quick, knowing glances as they crossed the river below the rugged rock face of the falls. Alicia and the visitors didn't notice.

They stuck to the path on the way up to the ridgeline, crossing a few deep gullies on rickety log bridges.

They found 16 chimpanzees, all sitting quietly up in the trees. Many were chewing wadges, which they would periodically remove, examine, and replace in their mouths.

"Who do we have?" asked Alicia.

"I don't see Stone, Chicken, or Mango," said Peter, as he began to write down their observations.

"Dr. Alicia," said Ja, pointing toward the ground just next to them.

The body of a three-foot long snake lay on the ground. It was dead, and the lower half of the body had been picked clean of flesh. The snake's bones and spine, still intact, glistened a translucent white.

Elizabeth squealed and jumped back.

"It's dead," said Peter, "but don't touch it."

"Is it poisonous?" she asked.

Peter knew it was not venomous but deferred to Ja with a glance.

"Not poison," said Ja.

"There's no flies," said Alicia, "and it doesn't stink. It's not been dead for long."

"Look how those bones are picked clean," said Peter. "Like a person ate a fish."

"Somebody ate it for sure, but who?" asked Alicia

"Somebody killed it, very recently," added Peter, as he took out his camera and began to snap pictures.

"Can I take pictures of it?" asked Whitney.

"Sure," said Alicia.

"Maybe a serval or a jackal killed it," said Peter.

"They would not pick the bones clean," said Alicia. "They'd just eat it bones and all."

"Maybe a hawk or eagle?"

"They would have carried the snake off and eaten it up in a tree," reasoned Alicia. "Anyway, this is what they were screaming about. Chimps *hate* snakes."

"Chimp kill snake. Chimps eat snake," said Ja.

"Not possible," said Alicia. "Chimps run away from snakes."

"These chimps eat snakes," insisted Ja. "Only this kind. Black snake. Not poison."

The thought slammed into Alicia's brain. The Gishwati chimps, confined in this small forest, had barely enough to eat. She wondered: *Could they overcome their fear of snakes to kill them and get some badly needed protein and nutrients?*

"Peter, this is a big deal," said Alicia. "Measure the snake, get good photos, including its head, before the flies show up."

"Are you sure it's not poisonous?" Alicia asked Ja.

"Not poison."

When Peter was done, Alicia carefully picked up the snake and put it into a plastic zip bag. The two younger women were too grossed out to watch, but too fascinated to look away.

"It's staring to stink now," said Alicia.

The chimpanzees barked and screamed as she tucked the snake in her pack.

"Sorry to interrupt your meal, guys, but I need this," said Alicia.

Alicia would later write up a report on the incident, with Peter and Ja as co-authors. The paper argued that, although the authors had not actually seen the kill, the chimpanzees had probably killed and eaten the snake. There was no other plausible explanation. No other chimpanzees had ever been seen killing or eating a snake, anywhere. Hunger, they reasoned, had driven the Gishwati chimpanzees to engage in such risky behavior. The report, when it was published, made a bit of a stir in chimpanzee scientific circles. Her grant manager at the Ark foundation was delighted.

"It's already one o'clock," said Alicia. "Let's go back down to the falls, have a bite, and head back. Augustin is expecting you two by two-thirty. You've seen some really cool stuff today."

Chapter 26) Long Call

The Kazaneza Falls are approximately 35 feet high. When it rains hard, the water pours over the falls in a deafening, brownish, 25 foot-wide torrent. During dry spells, the water flows placidly over the edge, like a stream of clear water poured from a pitcher, only a few feet wide. The rocky face to the left and right of the falls is gnarled with rock protrusions that have been worn smooth by water and spray over the years. Several species of ferns and air-breathing plants cling tenaciously to fissures among the rocks, forming lush green accents.

"Sometimes you can't hear yourself talk," said Peter, as he and Alicia ate hard-boiled eggs and Whitney ate a power bar. Elizabeth was not hungry. Peter had brought two eggs and a piece of cheese for Ja as well. Ja gladly accepted and went off by himself to eat.

"Too bad you guys didn't get to see Stone, the alpha male," said Alicia.

"You did see Fig, one of the big boys, but the other three, Stone, Chicken, and Mango, were not at the snake kill," said Peter.

"Doesn't really matter," said Alicia. "The females run the show anyway. Must have been a female that had the guts to kill the snake."

"I wonder where the boys are?" mused Peter. "They're quiet too."

"Must be scheming," said Alicia, with a smile.

She had no idea how right she was.

"It's so exotic," said Whitney. "If this were a movie, there'd be a romantic cave behind the falls."

"Nope, no cave," said Alicia. "Just a wall of slimy rock."

Alicia was correct: there was no cave *behind* the waterfall.

"Let's get moving," said Alicia, as they all took drinks of water.

The step up to the trail from the riverbed was several vertical feet of slimy mud and slippery roots. Peter enjoyed giving the young women a boost from behind.

They climbed up to the ridge top on the other side.

Elizabeth caught up to Alicia, her face pale.

"Um, I've got to go," Elizabeth said, her face now reddening.

"It's OK. Come with me," offered Alicia, signaling to Peter to remain with Whitney.

"Long call or short call?" asked Alicia as she walked Elizabeth down the path.

"What?" she replied.

"Do I have to dig a deep hole or a shallow hole?"

"Oh, a deep one," Elizabeth replied, her face now scarlet with embarrassment.

Alicia took two steps off the path, found a small opening, and dug a foot-deep hole with her machete. She produced a small roll of toilet paper from her pack, and set the machete on the ground next to the pile of excavated dirt.

"Just fill the hole when you're done, take a left on the trail and we'll be waiting for you. Don't worry. It happens to the best of us."

REI and Victoria's Secret were lowered unceremoniously as soon as Alicia had disappeared around the bend. Elizabeth was paying the price for too much bacon and coffee at breakfast this morning.

She found an unexpected peace, alone here, with the peeps of tree frogs and the droning of insects. She had no idea that others were watching.

Alicia, Whitney, and Peter sat on a log, just around the bend. Ja was gone, to re-contact the chimpanzees and follow them to their night nests.

"How did you end up studying chimpanzees in Rwanda, Dr. Oliveira?" Whitney asked Alicia.

"Alicia, please," the scientist responded. "I'm not really a doctor yet, and I'm barely older than you. "I'm Brazilian. I got a job helping some Smithsonian scientists reintroduce small monkeys, called golden lion tamarins, into the forest near Rio de Janeiro. I wanted to do primate field work all my life. I had read about Jane Goodall and Dian Fossey and wanted to study chimpanzees or gorillas in Africa. But you need a PhD to do that these days. I got a university scholarship, cruised through the coursework, and got a grant to do my doctoral thesis on the feeding behavior of the Gishwati chimpanzees, and here I am."

"Cool."

Alicia omitted the spurned offer of marriage and changed the subject to Peter.

"Peter has lived here most of his life, more than 20 years. He knows every inch of the place, all of the plants, the animals, and everything about the chimpanzees. He even gave them their names. He's been the voice of the forest, arguing for its protection. He's the one who should be getting the doctorate."

Peter was blushing as he fished a small bottle of hand sanitizer out of his pack, in anticipation of Elizabeth's return. "Yeah, but I'd never seen the chimps eat a snake... that's a first for me," he said. "She should be back by now."

"She can hardly be fixing her makeup," added Whitney.

Elizabeth had topped off the hole with dirt, stepped on the path, and turned left.

Stone faced her, not menacingly. Elizabeth's stomach churned, but not from bacon and coffee this time.

She turned, to see Chicken and Fig behind her, and then saw Mango in the clearing.

Stone walked toward her. She could smell his fruity presence, the result of his feeding on figs and flowers.

Elizabeth turned and retreated. Mango cut off her retreat, and Chicken and Fig moved up to flank her. She had nowhere to go but to follow Stone downhill, off the trail and through the undergrowth. She thought about brandishing the machete but realized that she wouldn't actually cut one of these animals unless it was threatening her. She took a few steps, and the males advanced in formation. She took a few steps more, and the males followed. She could hear the river gurgling below.

Mango was obsessing about the bare behind he had seen so recently. Different from a chimpanzee's but even more exciting.

Stone's glare told Mango not to dare to touch this girl. Stone was planning to use Elizabeth to get Bee back, and he needed her to be unharmed.

Chapter 27) The Missing Tourist

Alicia, Peter, and Whitney backtracked cautiously toward the clearing where Alicia had left Elizabeth. They did not want to walk in on her if she was still using the latrine. They called her name. There was no response.

"She must have turned the wrong way and walked in the other direction on the trail," said Peter. "You stay here and I'll jog ahead and catch up to her."

"I'll call her," said Whitney, pulling her phone out of her pack. "Crap, no bars, no service."

Peter saw the knuckle-prints and footprints of the chimpanzees in the mud, just off the trail. He noted that there was sign of more than one chimpanzee, but he couldn't tell how many.

The males must have been here this morning, he thought. *Ja would know who and how many and when. I wish he would carry a radio.*

"Any sign of her?" Alicia asked over the radio after 10 minutes.

"Nothing, not even a boot print," crackled Peter's voice over the walkie-talkie.

"I'll walk the other way. Keep calling her name," said Alicia.

"Would she be hiding on us, playing a trick or something?" Alicia asked Whitney.

"No way. She's terrified of snakes and lizards and bugs. It took all of her courage to even come here with you. She'd never stay alone."

"She's no more than 60 minutes from the edge of the forest, whichever way she walks," said Alicia. "And people will help her when she does come out. Don't worry."

But it was Alicia who was worried.

"Does she take any medication or drugs that would make her pass out or get confused?" Alicia asked.

"Nothing," said Whitney confidently.

"Maybe she slipped past us somehow and went back to the field station," said Alicia, hopefully.

"Keep looking, Peter. We're going back to the field station to see if she's there," said Alicia over the radio.

"Ten-four."

Chapter 28) Elizabeth is Missing

Augustin was sleeping in the rear seat of the Land Cruiser when Alicia and Whitney arrived at the field station.

"Wake up. Elizabeth is missing," said Alicia.

"What do you mean 'missing'?" asked Augustin.

"We left her alone near a trail for a few minutes because she needed to go. She never came back, and we haven't found her."

"Who is looking for her?"

"We searched for an hour, and my field assistant is still out there."

"Whitney, do you know anything about this?" asked Augustin.

"No. It's just like Dr. Oliveira said."

"What now?" asked Augustin.

"I don't know. Maybe we should just wait an hour? It's 3 now and it won't be dark until 5. She'll probably stumble out of the forest in a few minutes. People will bring her back."

"I've got to call my office," said Augustin. He stepped into the street and made a call.

Whitney also found a connection and tweeted: "Elizabeth is lost in the Gishwati Forest." Whitney had a few hundred followers, most of whom had been enjoying her Twitter and Facebook messages about her and Elizabeth's travels in Rwanda. She didn't have any followers in Rwanda yet, except Mrs. Kimberley Weatherby, who was in a meeting in Kigali and was not checking messages.

Alicia was trying to remember when and where she last saw Ja. *He could find Elizabeth if anybody could,* she thought.

Augustin returned. "My office said to call the police if Elizabeth is not back by 4."

Shit, thought Alicia. "Leonard, please make us all some coffee. It's going to be a long afternoon."

Alicia started to enumerate the possibilities in her mind:

Lost. She's got some food and water and a jacket, and my machete. She'll make it through the night.

Injured or ill. We'll find her tomorrow. She'll be OK if she's not bleeding out.

Kidnapped by the poachers. Going for a big ransom this time. They could have come in from the east side.

Kidnapped by some locals, to make their point about how the chimpanzees are endangering their babies and raiding their crops.

The first two were the most likely, and would turn out OK. The kidnap options were more serious, especially if the poachers were involved.

Four o'clock came quickly.

"Any sign of her?" Alicia asked Peter over the radio.

"Nothing," he answered.

"Is Ja with you?"

"No, he left us at the waterfall to follow the chimps."

Lieutenant Habimana's suspicions flowed back into Alicia's

mind.

"OK, I'll call," said Alicia. She dialed the lieutenant's cell phone directly.

Before she could say more than hello, he said: "I've closed the case. There's too much crime up here to search for a stolen chimpanzee."

"It's even worse than that this time," she said, and told him what had happened.

"What do you mean 'missing'?" he asked.

"Gone, disappeared, for almost three hours now."

"You better call Minister Olivier. He won't want to be blind-sided."

Rwanda's Minister of Natural Resources, Olivier Kanoro, was Alicia's official point of contact. They were not fond of each other. The minister resented her direct connection with H.E. She disagreed with his belief that "natural resources" were all to be harvested and mined for the economic betterment of Rwanda's people.

"The minister is not available," said his secretary. "Can I give him a message?"

"Please tell him that a student disappeared in the Gishwati Forest this afternoon."

"A Rwandan student?"

"No, an American."

Alicia's phone rang a minute after she had disconnected.

"What's going on up there?" asked the minister.

"An American student disappeared in the forest this afternoon."

"Was she working with you?"

"She was a tourist."

"Name?"

"Elizabeth Weatherby."

"Any relation to the woman from Gaslight?" asked the minister. He was also the official point of contact for Kimberly Weatherby and had negotiated the contract with Gaslight International to make electricity from the methane in Lake Kivu.

"Her daughter, I think," said Alicia.

"What are you doing to find her?"

"I've notified the Rutsiro District police, and my staff is looking for her."

"Stay with your phone. I've got to make some calls."

As the Minster hung up, Kim Weatherby was checking her messages. She saw Whitney's Tweet: "Elizabeth is lost in the Gishwati Forest." The mother, not thinking that her daughter could literally be lost, was pleased to learn that her daughter was mesmerized by a Rwandan rainforest.

Chapter 29) Cat Unleashed

Madam Chen had brought some food to Bee and the serval in the early afternoon. Bee got a black, overripe avocado and Cat, as Bee had begun to think of him, got a waxy rind of cheese. Bee left some avocado for Cat.

Cat felt a little peppy after lunch and poked Bee with his long front limb. Bee was impressed with the softness of his paw. She had no idea of the frighteningly sharp claws that were retracted within. Bee did a pirouette and tugged on Cat's leg. Cat jumped straight up into the air from all fours, and landed atop Bee, mouthing her gently, and then rolled over on his back. Bee thumped him resoundingly and ran, forgetting that she was tied up. She hit the end of her chain and was jerked backward. The play was over. Bee went into one of the boxes and sulked. Cat crawled into, actually onto, her lap and curled up.

Bee began to fidget with Cat's collar, which was just a slipknot made of rope. Cat, of course, lacked the fingers to hold the loop and slip the rope backward to loosen the knot. Bee had the fingers but didn't yet understand how slipknots worked. She fidgeted with the loop and the rope. Cat objected when she pulled the knot tighter, and his muscles relaxed when Bee played with the rope in a way that loosened the knot. Bee had gotten to like Cat, and liked him "relaxed" more than "objecting". So she unconsciously began to "loosen" more than "tighten" as she fidgeted. She finally ended up with a big loop and, as Cat raised his head sleepily in response to a sound outside, his head simply slipped through the knot. He was free, but he didn't know it yet. He dropped his head and fell asleep again.

Bee slipped the rope around her wrist and the knot tightened as she raised her arm. She could understand how that might hurt. She loosened the knot and slipped it off her arm. Then she too went to sleep.

Cat woke up first, walked out of the box and stretched. He walked to the end of his rope to the distant spot that he had chosen as a latrine. Something was different. He pooped and walked back. There was no rope dragging behind him.

Bee awoke to find Cat staring at her intently. She sensed a moment of change. Cat walked to the base of the wall beneath the little, partly open window and leapt six feet straight up to the sill. He grabbed on with extended claws, which Bee noticed for the first time, stood briefly on the sill, and then disappeared into the darkening evening.

Bee had lost her only friend.

Chapter 30) Another Prisoner

Elizabeth was also making some new friends, or at least

acquaintances. The walk downhill was difficult, but her chimpanzee escorts were patient. They didn't actually help her, but they didn't push her too hard.

She yelled: "Help!"

Stone screamed immediately. Peter heard the scream and noted that the males, whom he had not seen earlier, were now down by the Pfunda.

Elizabeth reasoned that now she really was being threatened and could cut one of the apes with the machete, but the others would probably hurt her in retaliation.

She yelled again and Stone screamed again, successfully masking Elizabeth's call.

Must be a squabble, thought Peter.

The water in the Pfunda was still low, forcing Elizabeth to scramble down the steep bank to get to the water. She put the machete down, turned onto her stomach, held on to some roots, let her legs dangle over the bank, and dropped to a rock below. Once she was down, the bank was too high for her to reach up to the machete. Stone, following close behind, made sure that she did not climb back up to get it. The machete was lost, at least to Elizabeth.

Chicken, Fig, and Mango crossed the Pfunda in overhead branches. Stone, who like most chimpanzees, did not like to wade or swim, found a suspended log from which he could keep Elizabeth moving. She stepped from slippery rock to slippery rock until she reached the other side. The bank here was impossibly steep and high.

Stone hefted the log and propped it at an angle from the riverbed to the top of the bank. He walked up it effortlessly and expected Elizabeth to do the same. She turned and made a dash for the other side of the river. Stone hopscotched across the riverbed and met her there, looking cross. They stood facing each other, he on all fours and she standing in soaked boots on a rock. Time stopped; the Pfunda gurgled at their feet in its eternal flow. Elizabeth sighed, turned, and recrossed. This time, she gracelessly climbed up the angled log to top of the far bank.

The group changed course and began to move upstream. The sound of the falls grew louder as they moved closer, becoming too loud for her cries for help to be heard, even without Stone's interference.

She could see glimpses of the falls in the gathering dusk and feel the water's coolness in the air. Finally, they were beside the torrent. The apes herded her upward into the forest on the side of the falls that was to the right as one faced the falling water.

The climb was steep. Elizabeth was crawling upward, scrabbling on hands and knees, sweating. The apes stopped three-quarters of the way up the steep slope, and then began to herd her sideways, toward the falls. They inched out of the forest, and Elizabeth saw only rock and rushing water ahead.

Stone moved to the front and stepped into a thin crack that ran horizontally through the rock face toward the falls. He turned and offered Elizabeth his hand. She hesitated. He grabbed her hand and began to lead her across the rock, her feet searching for toeholds in the crack. She could not have made the traverse on her own.

The crack led to a hollow in the rock face, about three feet high and a foot across. Stone stooped and stepped into the hollow, still pulling Elizabeth gently along. He eased her into the narrow space. The two hunched over, their bodies momentarily squeezed together. The riverbed was 25 feet below them.

Stone backed up, seeming to melt deeper into the crevice. She saw a darkened opening and took a step forward. Fig slipped in to the space behind her in the hollow. The opening was small. Elizabeth had to get on her hands and knees to get through.

She found herself in a cave that was as big as a house tent. The walls were rippled and folded, and arched upward to form a rounded ceiling that was five feet high. The floor was flat, wet in places and dry in others. A few odd chunks of rock that had fallen from the ceiling over the years littered the floor. Water trickled down the walls in a few small streams. Some of the stone appeared to be soft and flaky and some was hard rock. There were some shiny flecks in the soft stuff, sparkling even in the subdued light of the cave.

Elizabeth had to stoop to stand. Chicken, Fig, and Mango all entered the cave soundlessly. There was not an arm's length between any of them and Elizabeth.

The apes were used to being close to humans they trusted. They often fed close to Peter and Alicia as the observers took notes on their behavior. Bee and Potato sometimes tried to touch the people. While it was not unusual for the chimpanzees to be close to people, it was a first, an unsettling first, for Elizabeth to be so close to apes. But she now knew that the chimpanzees were not going to hurt her. If that had been their intent they would not have brought her all the way here.

I'm in a chimpanzee jail! Why? What are they going to do now?

Despairing and physically exhausted, Elizabeth sat down on a dry spot on the floor of the cave, her arms and head on folded knees. She began to sob. Tears welled in her eyes and rolled down her cheeks. The chimpanzees did not recognize crying as an expression of sadness.

But Mango wanted to lick those salty tears. It was not only the salt. All the salt he could eat in a lifetime was a step away in the veins of soft clay in the walls of the cave. This was, after all, Clay Cave, where chimpanzees and Rwandans have been coming for millennia to lick and gouge out the extra minerals that were so essential to their health. The Batwa still gathered salt here.

No, Mango was stirred by something other than salt in the tears of this beautiful but now helpless blond human.

Stone saw Mango's perverse interest. The old male's hair

began to stiffen and he stared directly at Mango. Mango got the message. Even Elizabeth sensed the confrontation.

Chicken and Fig hurriedly squeezed out of the cave. Mango glanced at Elizabeth, then at Stone, then back at Elizabeth, and exited reluctantly.

Stone followed and sat in the outside fissure, his massive back to Elizabeth. His eyes met another's, far downstream. Ja had found the chimpanzees, at least the males. The girl had been a surprise; he had watched as the chimpanzees eased her into the cave.

Chapter 31) A Meager Supper

Augustin, Leonard, Alicia, and Whitney sat long-faced at the table in Mama Bernard's inn. Peter sat on the bench. Three half-empty bottles of Primus beer and glasses sat on the table. The air was tinged with smoke from two spluttering candles and from the fire that Mama had lit in her small kitchen to take the chill off the evening and to cook beans for her family's supper. Her son, sharing a chair with Leonard, sat at the table, pretending to do homework but actually lapping up every word that was spoken. This was the best English lesson any twelve year-old was going to get in Kinihira tonight.

Lieutenant Habimana joined them at 7. By 9, he had interviewed each of them, separately, in the field station.

There were no discrepancies in their stories. A healthy, fit, sane American girl had disappeared in the Gishwati Forest at about 1:30 that afternoon. Peter, Alicia, and Whitney could each attest that none of the others had had the opportunity to be involved in the disappearance. Augustin and Leonard vouched for each other's being at the field station during the entire afternoon. There were no animals in the Gishwati Forest that could have eaten her, no lakes in which she could have drowned, no quicksand. Habimana concluded that she was either injured or ill in the forest, or she had been kidnapped. The missing girl did come from a wealthy family.

The five witnesses also agreed on two other facts: Elizabeth (or her captors) had taken Alicia's machete, and nobody knew where Ja had been during or after the disappearance.

The Batwa were once again awakened by a squad of armed police officers, this time in the middle of the night. The officers found banked, smoky fires in the Batwa huts. The sleeping people had red eyes and runny noses from the smoke, and there was a pungent smell of banana beer in the huts. The police dumped blankets, bedding, and housewares out of the huts into the cold, damp night. The huts were otherwise empty. Ja was not home.

The officers notified Habimana by phone of their failure to find a trace of Ja or Elizabeth. He instructed them to head home and be prepared to widen the search in and around the forest the next day.

He called Minister Kanoro to report the news.

"Put every officer on the search tomorrow," the minister

ordered. "Your chief has been informed. Search every house around the forest, and set up a roadblock on the road down the mountain. I informed the girl's mother yesterday of her daughter's disappearance, and she has already called H.E."

After he disconnected, Habimana faced the small group. "I'll want you two to go into the forest with my people tomorrow," he said, nodding to Peter and Alicia. "We'll be looking for Elizabeth and for Ja. Have you looked through the camera traps?"

Alicia and Peter exchanged guilty looks. "We never put them back out after Apple was killed and Bee was kidn... uh, stolen."

"You take the girl back to Kigali in the morning," he ordered Augustin.

"No way. I want to stay here," said Whitney.

"Mrs. Weatherby wants you to come back."

"She's not my mother."

"She'll probably want to come up here anyway," Habimana relented.

"But your boss wants you and the car back in Kigali," he told Augustin.

"I'll leave now."

"Check the Toyota before he goes," Habimana told a uniformed officer.

Habimana then turned to Mama Bernard, who had joined her son at the spectator's end of the table. "I need you to make food for my people tomorrow – beans, eggs, cheese, bread, *mandazi,* cake – and have drinkable water too."

Mama Bernard walked into the street, flipped open her phone, and called her sister in Gisenyi. She gave her a shopping list and a promise of a share of the profits if she bought everything and put it on the first bus up the mountain in the morning.

"Dr. Oliveira, I'll want to use your field station as a headquarters," he said to Alicia. "You can stay there but you're going to have lots of company. I'm at least looking forward to more of your coffee. This should all be over by tomorrow night."

Augustin turned the Land Cruiser out of the gate and headed down the mountain. Habimana and his driver headed off in the opposite direction.

"Can we go home too?" asked Peter, Leonard at his side.

"I left you some beans and warm water," said Leonard.

"Be back early, OK?" said Alicia.

Whitney and Alicia walked back to the field station in the cool, quiet night. A few candles and now-dwindling cooking fires flickered in the still night of Kinihira village.

Alicia showed Whiney how to take a field station shower, and loaned her a set of sweats and a pair of dry socks for the night.

"I want to try to put something on Facebook," said Whitney.

"About Elizabeth?" asked Alicia.

"Yeah."

"Hold on, let's think this through. What do we want to say?" said Alicia. "I need to protect my work and this forest and these chimpanzees."

"Wow, I hadn't thought of that," said Whitney.

"You know, we could work together," said Alicia. "There won't be any media people up here. You can cover the story... an exclusive... and help me protect the place."

"From what?" asked Whitney.

"Not exactly sure yet but I think there will be trouble over this."

"Deal," said Whitney. They picked at bowls of now-cooled beans and crashed in Alicia's bed.

Chapter 32) Another Meager Supper

It was intuitively obvious to Cat that everybody would be happy with a fresh dead rat. He placed it ceremoniously in front of Bee, with what some would say was a flush of pride. Bee was impressed and might have eaten some, but she did not know how to get into it, how to tear it apart. Stone had always done that part for her.

Cat had returned in the early evening through the same small window as he had left. The city had been terrifying. Bee had been in a mopey sleep when her supper had been delivered, and was happier to see Cat than the rat.

The door to the back room opened, and Cat leapt on to Bee's lap and hid his head and neck under Bee's arm. Bee had the slipknot in her hand, and Madam Chen did not notice that Cat was actually unattached. She threw a sticky black banana at Bee, and refilled the can of water.

After Chen returned to the store, Bee ate the banana and Cat ate the rat. They played for a little while, and fell asleep in one of the crates. Cat was unable to share his adventures in the city of Gisenyi. Bee was thinking about how to open a dead rat.

Chapter 33) Yet Another Meager Supper

Rain appeared 30 minutes after Chicken, Fig, and Mango had left. Stone sniffed and mounted her in greeting, and both entered the cave. Elizabeth stiffened.

This is a new one, she thought. *Why is its butt so big and pink? Oh, it's a female.*

Stone placed his hand protectively on Elizabeth's shoulder. Rain understood that he wanted her to take care of the girl, and summon him if there were trouble.

Stone left as the sun set. Rain lay down in the cave, a few feet from Elizabeth. Droplets of rain flecked Rain's hair. Her ears and face were splotched with pink and black skin and were more sparsely haired than the rest of her. Elizabeth was surprised that she wasn't dirty and didn't smell bad. She couldn't figure out the anatomical details of Rain's swollen, naked, pink butt.

Elizabeth finished one of her bottles of water. She unwrapped an energy bar and ate only half, choosing to ration what little food she had. She had an urge to offer the other half to Rain, but then decided that this was not a time for politeness.

Rain got up and left. Elizabeth inched through the cave's opening and looked out into the gathering darkness. Running for it now was out of the question, or was it? Her deliberation was interrupted by Rain's return. Rain had an enormous armload of leafy branches. She pushed her way into the cave and began breaking up the branches and arranging them into a bowl-like form. She lined it with the leafy boughs, weaving them in and out, securely into place. Rain climbed in and lay down.

Elizabeth took off her vest and pulled a long-sleeved compression shirt out of one of the larger pockets. She felt too weird to take her field shirt off in front of this ape, even if she was a female. Instead, Elizabeth layered the compression shirt over her shirt and then put her vest back on. She felt her phone in one of the vest's pockets.

My phone! she thought. Her hopes soared. She turned it on. The battery was at 70% but there were no bars. One of the finest bits of modern technology was useless here. *Maybe outside?* she thought. *If I could get out again?*

She checked messages. Nothing. She smiled at the picture of the baby gorilla that she had attached to a message to her mother yesterday.

Mom will send people to find me. Turn it off, conserve power. Still hungry, but save food.

Rain interrupted Elizabeth's stream of thoughts by getting up abruptly and leaving again. She returned a few minutes later with another armload of branches, and put them down in front of Elizabeth.

Are these for me? thought Elizabeth. *Could she have brought these for me?*

Rain slid her hand into the fold between her inner thigh and her abdomen, and brought out a handful of small fruits that she had carried there. These too she placed in front of Elizabeth.

Rain was puzzled that Elizabeth neither made a nest nor ate the fruit.

But Rain's little sister, Bee, also didn't know how to make

a nest or which fruit was safe to eat. Rain saddened at the thought of her missing sister, but Stone had given her a task.

Just as she would for Bee's mid-day nap, Rain began to build a nest for Elizabeth. She even took some leaves from her own bed to make Elizabeth's softer. Rain whimpered at Elizabeth, and lay down in her own now-slightly-less-soft bed.

Elizabeth was astounded at this gesture of kindness. She was ashamed now that she had not offered this new "friend" a bit of energy bar.

How can I have an ape as a friend? This is too weird.

But Elizabeth did climb into the bed, which Dr. Oliveira had called a nest, and lay down. It was surprisingly comfortable, and she soon felt the warmth of her body that was being trapped beneath her. What had Dr. Oliveira told her about chimpanzee nests?

One ape to a nest except for a mother with her baby. New nest every night and noontime. Simpler nest at noon than at night.

Rain reached over, picked up one of the little fruits, and put it into her mouth. Elizabeth imitated. The fruit was sour but not unpleasant, and it was juicy. Rain ate three of the six that remained, and Elizabeth ate the other three. They both fell asleep.

Chapter 34) The Search for Elizabeth, Day 2

A squad of 16 Rutsiro police officers pulled up in two pickups in front of the field station at 7 a.m. Peter, Whitney and Alicia were finishing their simple breakfast. Whitney liked the igikoma. Alicia made two extra cups of coffee in her press.

Lieutenant Habimana's driver honked his horn, and Leonard rushed out to open the field station gate. Mama Bernard stood expectantly in the doorway of her inn across the street. A few villagers gathered to see what the police wanted.

Habimana told his officers to get their breakfasts and lunches at the inn. Mama and her son distributed bowls of igikoma made with fresh goats' milk to the first eight officers, washed the bowls and spoons, and then fed the other eight. Each officer got a "lunchbox" containing two fried mandazi grain cakes, a wedge of Gishwati cheese, two hard-boiled eggs and two small bananas. The lunchboxes were actually two sheets of carefully folded newspaper, since plastic bags are outlawed in Rwanda. Mama's son handed each officer a bottle of water.

The police were dressed in camos and boots, and each carried an AK-47. Few of them were looking forward to spending their day in the forest. Rumors were now flying among the villagers, the most popular of which was that a chimpanzee had killed a farmer's baby.

Habimana greeted Alicia and her team somberly in the

dining room and gratefully accepted a cup of Alicia's coffee. He was in street clothes, clearly not intending to accompany his officers into the forest.

"We have two objectives," he began. "First is to find and rescue Elizabeth and second is to arrest Ja. We think this is a kidnapping, and Ja is really the only person who was at the scene, has no alibi, and who could capture the girl and bring her out of the forest. He's poor and could use the ransom money."

"There is another sixteen-person team that is already searching houses, starting with houses closest to the forest and working outward. We're also setting up a roadblock on the road."

"What if she's already gone?" asked Whitney.

"Unlikely," he answered. Alicia and Peter immediately thought of how quickly Bee had disappeared.

"She may still be in the forest, injured, ill, or a captive. Peter, I want you to take eight officers to the spot where Elizabeth disappeared. They will fan out from there. Dr. Oliveira, I'd like you to take the other eight to the east side of the reserve and work back toward us. Two officers in each team have walkie-talkies. Take yours too, and tune them to our frequency."

"Oh, and one more thing. The officers have orders to shoot Ja in the legs if he tries to run away."

The field team was appalled, but Peter knew that if Ja were still in the forest, he would not let himself be seen.

The four of them walked to the street. Habimana repeated the plan to the officers. His streetside briefing also ended the rumors among the onlooking villagers. They now knew that a search was on for a missing American girl. The locals were surprised that none among them had heard anything about an American girl; she would have been difficult to hide in this close-knit community.

Leonard told Peter and Alicia to get lunches from Mama. They were out of food at the field station. Two more checks on Mama's invoice.

"Get a lunch and come with me," Alicia told Whitney.

"No, she stays here," said Habimana. "I don't want another missing girl, and she needs to be here anyway to meet Mrs. Weatherby."

Alicia moved unobtrusively next to Habimana as the officers stuffed their lunches into their pockets. "Do we really have to shoot him?"

"Those are Kigali's orders," said Habimana.

Alicia walked over to Whitney. "Keep it short and simple. Elizabeth has been missing for 18 hours. A police search is underway. We are confident that she will be found."

"I'm not," said Whitney.

"Not what?"

"Not confident."

"OK, drop the 'confident' part. Use 'expecting' or 'hoping'."

Alicia and Peter did exactly as they had been directed. None of the officers was willing to go off-trail, so there was no "fanning out" from the spot from which Elizabeth had disappeared. Peter had already walked all of the trails. He knew that there would be no sign of her.

Alicia's team crossed the Gumba on the log. The officers crossed easily. They would have been steadier on bare feet than in their heavy boots, because they were Rwandans, and Rwandans learn from infancy how to cross rivers barefoot on fallen logs. Most of them were huffing and sweating by the time they climbed the ridge that overlooked the Pfunda. Their guns were no help for deflecting overhanging branches and thorns. Alicia realized the importance of Ja's keeping these trails open. The forest can reclaim them in days.

Alicia led her team down the ridge and across the Pfunda at a point that was less than 100 feet upstream from the falls. The raging water stifled their conversations. Elizabeth was unaware of their presence.

Both teams informed Habimana of their movements and lack of any progress at 11 a.m. He told them to keep searching.

Chapter 35) Escalation

The Eco-Trek Land Rover, somehow still shiny after the ten-hour round trip to and from Kigali, pulled up to the field station at 11:30 a.m. Augustin blew the horn at the closed gate. Leonard opened it. Now there was a throng of villagers in the street.

Augustin pulled the SUV into the field station driveway behind the police sedan and did not have time to open the passenger-side door before Mrs. Kimberly Weatherby stepped out.

She was smartly but simply dressed in the field clothes and boots that she wore when she visited Gaslight's methane extracting stations on Lake Kivu and the electrical generating plants on the shore.

"Who's in charge here?" she asked Leonard.

"Dr. Oliveira. She's in the forest now,"

"Who's in the police car?"

"Lieutenant Habimana. Rutsiro district. In the dining room."

"I'm Kimberley Weatherby. It's my daughter who's missing," Weatherby told Habimana as she entered the dining room.

"Sorry this happened."

"Where are we?" she asked the lieutenant.

"We have two teams searching the forest for Elizabeth and for a local pygmy who may know something. We also have a squad searching houses around the forest. You must have passed through the roadblock on the way up."

"They weren't stopping cars that were driving up the mountain, only down."

"We don't know if this is an accident or there's foul play, but there's no sign of her so far," the lieutenant said.

"So, you have only a few local police on this?"

"Thirty-two to be precise."

"Dogs?"

"Ma'am, you must have noticed by now that we don't have many dogs in Rwanda, and we do not use them in police work. People here hate them. The genocide."

"She has an iPhone with a locator beacon. Have you tried to pick that up?"

"We don't have the equipment to do that. And, there have been no calls or texts that we're aware of."

"Helicopters? Radar?" she asked.

"A person can walk from one edge of this forest to the opposite edge in two hours, tops. No need for helicopters. Would you like a cup of coffee?" asked the lieutenant.

"Please."

"Leonard, can you bring me some hot water and coffee? I'll try the press."

Whitney walked into the dining room. She and Mrs. Weatherby hugged. There were a few tears.

"Take a walk with me," Weatherby asked Whitney.

Once outside, she said: "Tell me the whole story, beginning to end." Whitney complied. Mrs. Weatherby learned nothing that she had not already heard from Minister Kanoro, Augustin, and Habimana.

"I put out a Facebook message and a Tweet this morning," said Whitney.

"I saw it. Bare bones."

"We're trying to keep the emotional level down," said Whitney.

"Well, my emotional level is pretty high."

Another Toyota, this one a silver 4Runner, nosed its way through the gate but there was no room left in the driveway. The driver, who was armed, opened the rear door for Minister Olivier Kanoro.

Habimana left the dining room to greet this visitor. Kanoro was technically not his boss, but a district police officer readily took orders from a member of H.E.'s cabinet.

"Status?" asked Kanoro.

Habimana described what was being done to find Elizabeth.

Chapter 36) A Call for Help

Nothing had changed by 3 p.m. The minister ordered his driver to drive him down the mountain to the comforts of the Serena Hotel on the shore of Lake Kivu in Gisenyi. He had asked Habimana for hourly telephone updates.

The police search teams ended their work at 4. Alicia returned to the field station with them. Peter decided to hang back and "check on the behavior of the chimpanzees."

Kimberly Weatherby watched the police return from the forest empty-handed. Neither Habimana nor Alicia could provide any further information about Elizabeth. She picked up her phone. It was 9 a.m. in the Manhattan office of former United States President Bill Clinton.

"Thank you for taking my call, Mr. President. You may not remember me."

"Of course I remember you, Kim," said Clinton.

Gaslight International was a generous supporter of the Clinton Foundation's international charitable work, and the Weatherbys had contributed personally to both of Clinton's presidential campaigns.

"I hear your daughter is missing," Clinton continued.

"That was fast. We're half a world away and she's only been missing for a day," said Weatherby.

"There is a short piece in this morning's *Wall Street Journal*."

Weatherby briefly recalled Whitney's tweet, and went on: "That's why I'm calling Mr. President. The investigation here seems half-hearted and disorganized. You're a personal friend of President Kagame. Could you by any chance ask him to intervene and get a real search underway? We don't have much time."

"Do the police suspect that she was kidnapped?"

"Either kidnapped, or laying out there in the forest, injured or sick. Either way, we're running out of time."

Clinton had a daughter. He felt her pain.

"I'll call him. No promises though."

"Thank you, Mr. President."

Kagame took the call from his long-time friend and supporter at 5 p.m., Kigali time.

"I'll see what I can do, Mr. President."

"Thank you, Your Excellency."

Chapter 37) Elizabeth's Day

Rain had awakened at dawn and left the cave briefly to poop and pee from a nearby overhanging branch. When she returned, she beckoned Elizabeth to exit the cave and do the same. But Elizabeth could go only as far as the fissure in the rock face. She couldn't grab a branch or climb up or down the rock. She balanced at the edge of the fissure as well as she could. Her trickle joined a dozen rivulets of water that slid down the rock face next to the falls.

Another chimpanzee showed up at 8 a.m. Rain left. Both chimpanzees were aware that dozens of people were entering the forest.

Elizabeth saw that her new guard was also a female, perhaps a little older than the first.

Carrot had arrived on three limbs. She carried a melon-sized avocado in the fourth limb, her right hand. It was gleaming green and flecked with the black spots that told of perfect ripeness. Carrot had stolen it from a tree next to a farmer's house in the early morning.

Carrot offered the avocado to Elizabeth, who had learned in the past two weeks that Rwanda's huge avocados were the world's best. She took a small pocketknife from a vest pocket and cut sections from the fruit. She offered one to Carrot, who took it uncertainly. The two sat face-to-face on the cave floor and shared a breakfast.

Alicia and Peter had a policy against feeding the apes

because giving them human food would distort Alicia's study of the chimpanzees' feeding behavior. Carrot's sharing the avocado with Elizabeth was a first.

Carrot could have just eaten the avocado, but she *knew* that Elizabeth was scared and hungry. Many scientists think that only humans can understand how another feels and be empathetic.

Elizabeth tried several times during the day to move to the cave entrance to try her phone, but Carrot blocked the way. She was hopelessly bored but otherwise well. She did a few yoga moves, which completely mystified Carrot. Elizabeth wondered if anybody was looking for her.

Why did they take me? It can't be ransom... they don't know about money. What are they going to do with me? That one male had a nasty look but the others have been nice to me. Are they saving me for some... ceremony?

Rain returned in the afternoon with a groin-pocketful of small fruits. Carrot slipped out after spending several minutes scanning the valley from the fissure.

Is this the one who stayed with me last night? Alicia wondered.

She made a mental note to study the chimpanzees' faces for distinguishing marks, as Dr. Oliveira had described. But Elizabeth knew, she sensed, this one's *personality*.

She's gentle, kind, serious for being so young, and somehow seems to be very sad, thought Elizabeth.

Chapter 38) A Message to Ja

Peter had been thinking about Ja for the past 24 hours. There was indeed a lot of evidence that Ja could have been involved in Bee's kidnapping and in Elizabeth's disappearance. But he still leaned toward Ja's innocence. Ja liked to have a little bit of money but would not know what to do with a lot. He was reclusive and would not be inclined to make elaborate plans with strangers. His wife, however, could have put him up to it.

Peter wanted to protect Ja from the police until they knew more about how Elizabeth had disappeared. If Ja were involved, Peter would help him surrender. He would not continue to help him hide in the forest. But people were often guilty until proven innocent in Rwanda, and Lieutenant Habimana had already decided that Ja was guilty, or at least that he knew what happened to the apes and the girl. Ja would be shot trying to escape or would be captured, interrogated roughly, and thrown in jail. Jail would be worse for Ja.

The police had not noticed that Peter had eaten only one egg and one mandazi cake during the lunch break in the forest. He had carefully refolded his newspaper lunchbox and put it in his pack. Again, nobody noticed because the squad was under orders to bring out the remains of their lunch, the eggshells, cheese rinds, water bottle, and the newspaper. They too stuffed newspaper back in their pockets after lunch.

When the sounds of the clomping police had subsided,

Peter called out Elizabeth's name. They had done this all day. No response.

He came to an intersection of two trails where he often met up with Ja in the morning. He buried the remains of his uneaten lunch beneath some leaves. Ja would at least have a solid meal and know that Peter was thinking about him.

As Peter left the forest, he saw the Eco-Trek Land Cruiser headed down the mountain and waved to Augustin and the woman in the passenger seat. They too were headed down the mountain to the luxurious Serena Hotel for the night.

Alicia had taken her shower and was sharing coffee in the field station dining room with Habimana and Whitney. Peter joined them.

"Your officers will never find her if she's in the forest. They walked single-file, gabbing loudly, back and forth on our trails. Sure, they called Elizabeth's name, but by this time she may not be able to hear them. You've got to get off-trail," she scolded.

"They are not trained for that," he responded, "but we'll see what we can do tomorrow."

"We'll be happy to lead them if you tell them they have to go," said Alicia. "Peter and I could have made more progress by ourselves."

"OK, we'll be back at 7 in the morning."

Habimana left word with Mama Bernard to be prepared again for the officers in the morning. She expectantly offered him the bill for the day's food and drink, but he waved her off and told her to wait until the search was over.

"We made the *Wall Street Journal* this morning," Whitney told the team after Habimana had left. "That newspaper is read everywhere."

"How do you know there was a story?" asked Alicia.

"Mrs. Weatherby told me. I guess she found it on her phone. Here, you can read it on mine."

"I better send an e-mail to the Ark Foundation. They fund this place," said Alicia.

After a pause, Whitney looked empathetically at Alicia: "So... I need to know what you want out of this."

"What do you mean, 'what do I *want*?'"

"Just that, in order of importance. If I'm going to do your PR, I need to know your goals."

Alicia felt a surge of resentment toward this inexperienced young woman, who seemed to be taking over. But Alicia had to concede that she had a point.

"First, I want Elizabeth found, safe and sound."

"Second, I want to get back to my work. That's it."

"What about Ja?" asked Whitney.

"Oh," said Alicia. "If he's somehow involved or responsible, he needs to be punished."

"If he's responsible, yes but just involved, no," Peter interrupted.

"How can he be involved but not responsible?" asked Whitney.

"There were millions involved in our genocide but far fewer were responsible," said Peter. "I don't think Ja did it but he may know things that we don't."

"I have to report that the police are seeking a 'person of interest' in tomorrow's release. It's not fair to say only that the police searched the forest and found nothing."

"Will you name him?" asked Peter.

"Not at this point," said Whitney.

"Will you ask Habimana what he wants out of this?" asked Alicia.

"Already have. He wants Elizabeth back safely and wants to see justice done to any and all of those who were responsible. Same with Mrs. Weatherby. So, Elizabeth's return is everybody's top priority but we are not quite in agreement about your project or about punishing the wrongdoers, if there are wrongdoers," Whitney summarized. "And... ," she hesitated, "... we're not all on the same page about Ja."

"I want to protect him," said Peter.

"At the expense of our project?" asked Alicia.

"We still don't even know if there was a crime," reminded Whitney. "I'll stick to hope for Elizabeth's return, the search, and a 'person of interest'. I'll make it clear that you are helping in the search."

She waited for a response but got only a shrug from Alicia.

"I wonder what Ja wants out of this," said Peter.

"Have we all given up on Bee?" Alicia asked the other three.

Now they shrugged.

Whitney went into the street to get the coverage she needed to post her Twitter and Facebook messages. She sent an e-mail directly to the writer of the *Wall Street Journal* article, and made sure the spelling of her name, 'Whitney (with an "e") Logan' was correct. A crowd gathered around her. Her screen glowed in the gathering dusk.

Chapter 39) A Message from Ja

Rain left at dusk to gather fresh leaves for their nests. Elizabeth had to go, and managed to balance herself in the fissure. She could not lean out quite far enough to be completely fastidious, but she still had a bit of Alicia's toilet paper. Alone, she searched for an escape route. She could not climb up, and was frightened to climb down the steep face. She might be able to ease along the tiny ridge of rock that ran across the rock face, but a slip would be disastrous.

Phone, she thought, fumbling in her pocket for the 5c. She turned it on. There was only 58% of battery life remaining because she had passed some time during the day looking at pictures. No bars, no G's. Her spirits dropped. She couldn't make a call and she didn't know if the GPS beacon in her phone could still transmit.

She went back into the cave. She had finished all of her bottled water, but she could scoop up a few drops from the clean, cold rivulets that dripped down the cave walls.

Rain returned with the leaves, and a wad of newspaper. She gave half of the leaves and the newspaper to Elizabeth. It was a local Gisenyi paper, printed in Kinyarwanda. Maybe she could look at the photos and try to translate some words.

Where did she get the paper? Elizabeth asked herself.

Wait, there's something in the newspaper. Elizabeth unwrapped the paper carefully. Inside was an egg, a greasy fried pancake of some sort, a bite or two of cheese and a banana.

Rain watched with interest.

She didn't find this on her own. It's not like the avocado. Somebody, some human, gave this to her or left it for her to find. There's somebody out there looking for me, or at least looking out for me!

Elizabeth was elated, and scared Rain with her fist pump and squeal of hopeful delight. Rain even squeaked a little cry of excitement.

Elizabeth cracked the egg, preparing to lick up the liquidy center, but it was hard-boiled. She offered half to Rain, who sniffed it and declined, preferring instead to chew on some of the leaves.

What the hell is wrong with me? thought Elizabeth. *I'm half-starved and sharing the food I have with apes. I need to start a diary.* She had a pen and notebook in her vest.

Ja had found some eggs of his own in the forest, but his were full of gristly unborn wild bird chicks. He had eaten a half-slice of bread and a bit of cheese with his uncooked birdy omelet. Afterward, he had brought the last of the wrapped lunch to where Stone was making his bed for the night. Stone had been the delivery ape.

Like the others, Ja and Stone also wanted Elizabeth returned safely, but not until justice was restored at Gishwati. They certainly had not forgotten about Bee.

Chapter 40) The Search for Elizabeth, Day 3

The two huge stake-body Mercedes trucks crawled up the mountain in the middle of the night, gearboxes grinding as they went between first and second. They never got to a higher gear. The 30 troops in the back of each truck lurched and bounced with every rut and pothole in the dirt road, but they were used to rough transport. These were two platoons from the Third Division of the Rwanda Defence Force, which is stationed in Gisenyi. They were trained to find and destroy armed rebels in the rugged forested mountains of western Rwanda and the eastern Democratic Republic of Congo. These men and women lived to go off-trail. The order to deploy to Gishwati had come from Kigali at 7 p.m. on the previous night.

The trucks pulled up to the soccer field that was the front yard of the Kinihira elementary school at 7 a.m. The soldiers jumped from the trucks and formed a perimeter around the field. Students that were arriving for school were told that there would be no classes this day, but none returned home. Instead, their parents joined them at the schoolyard to watch the soldiers. The troops were polite but vigilant.

The thudding sound of the arriving Mi-17 helicopter was first heard at 7:25, and became thunderous by 7:30 as it hovered over the soccer field. Dust began to fly and long grass waved beneath the whirling rotors. The troops stood immobile, facing outward, as the storm-cloud gray helicopter settled to the ground and its engine was shut down.

Like the people of Kinihira, the Gishwati chimpanzees had never heard a sound as loud as the arriving helicopter. They ran, terrified, falling, screeching, momentarily forgetting all ties of kinship and community. Potato clung fiercely to Squash as she crashed through the trees without any idea of where she was going. Rain and Elizabeth had heard the chaos even in the depth of Clay Cave. Elizabeth could guess that it was a helicopter and was elated. Rain had all she could do to stay put.

The two lieutenants that commanded the platoons approached the helicopter. The pilot and copilot, both second lieutenants in the Rwandan Air Force and both women, climbed down and met them. The flight engineer stayed inside.

Habimana had arrived at the field station at 7 a.m. with a contingent of police to continue the search. He was totally surprised by the arrival of the troops and the helicopter. He, Alicia, Peter, and Whitney headed to the school. The soldiers allowed only Habimana to pass and meet with the officers.

"We are taking over the search today," one of the lieutenants told Habimana. "Your people can continue to search houses in the surrounding villages. We have high-resolution aerial images and maps of the forest, and will be walking straight-line transects from east-to-west and north-to-south. The helicopter has a color video camera and an infrared heat-sensing camera. It will search the forest and the surrounding fields from above. If the girl is in there, dead or alive, we'll find her."

Habimana told the officers about the suspect, Ja, but could not provide a good description. They already had a picture of Elizabeth.

There was no barking of orders, distribution of breakfasts or lunches, or idle chitchat. Each of the soldiers knew his or her assignment on the search grid and each knew the schedule. Radios were checked, and they moved silently into the forest.

The apes, and just about every other animal had run, flown, or crawled to the far edge of the forest, but they would not be alone for long. Ja and Stone, both worried, took up hidden positions in trees from which to watch the invasion.

Chapter 41) A Casualty

Whitney, Alicia, and Peter started back to the field station and their uneaten breakfasts after the troops had disappeared into the forest.

Whitney was tweeting: "Rwanda's military joins search for Elizabeth Weatherby in the Gishwati Forest."

"How did the army get involved?" asked Alicia. "And a helicopter?"

"Probably the minister," said Peter. "There must be a lot of pressure to find Elizabeth."

"Well, it's important to find her, pressure or no pressure," said Whitney. "And the police were not doing a very good job."

Kim Weatherby and Olivier Kanoro were waiting at the field station when the three returned. The guests had refused Leonard's hospitable offer of breakfast and coffee.

"I hope you all realize what's happened here," said the minister. "That helicopter flew down from southern Sudan last night on direct orders from H.E. It was pulled out of service with the United Nations mission. It's usually rescuing victims of the civil war and tracking down rebel militias."

Mrs. Weatherby was silently impressed with her influence, but her daughter was still missing.

"If the girl is in that forest, we'll find her in the next few hours," said the minister. "We can only pray that she's safe."

He retired to his Toyota to make and take calls. Mrs. Weatherby joined the others for coffee.

"I guess it's not possible for us to go into the forest today," said Alicia. "I hope the chimps will be OK."

The waiting began. Peter tried to find the soldiers' radio frequency on his walkie-talkie but could not. They heard the helicopter take off and begin circling over the forest. They could also hear the chimpanzees screaming.

The minister's driver came to the dining room an hour later and asked Alicia to come outside, alone. He led her to the minister's car. Kanoro waited in the rear seat.

"Please get in, Dr. Oliveira," Kanoro asked.

"Where are we going?" she asked.

"Nowhere, at least not now. We need to talk," he said.

She got in. The driver closed the door. The car smelled of faux leather and after-shave.

"You and your project have caused a series of disruptions that have been costly and embarrassing to the Rwandan government," he began.

"But... "

"Please do not interrupt me," he commanded.

"You have been conducting your research without a proper permit. Your research visa has not yet been issued. It is illegal to conduct research in Rwanda without a research visa."

"But... "

"I am offering you the courtesy of this conversation," he snapped. "If you interrupt me again, I will terminate our talk."

She relented.

"You entertained tourists at Gishwati without authorization. Gishwati is a forest reserve, not a national park, not yet at least, and tourism is therefore not allowed."

Alicia knew that this was technically true but everybody was aware that tour companies had been advertising trips to see the Gishwati chimpanzees.

"I have been authorized to instruct you to discontinue your project and leave Rwanda. The reason is your disrespect for our laws and procedures."

Alicia's world reeled. *My dissertation, my whole career, is ruined. Peter and Leonard and Ja will lose their jobs. Who knows what will happen to the chimpanzees?*

"You have two weeks to wrap things up and leave the country. Otherwise you will be detained and deported."

"Of course… " he went on, "we are assuming that you and your staff are not responsible for the Weatherby girl's disappearance. The consequences will be more serious if that is found to be untrue. And one last thing: don't try to appeal to H.E. He supports this decision."

Alicia noticed the word "support." It meant that Kanoro had been the one who *made* the decision. He had taken advantage of the situation to rid himself of an annoyance, and was setting Alicia up as a scapegoat if Elizabeth were not found safely. But he was right that an appeal to H.E. would be useless; Kanoro had obviously already gotten H.E.'s approval.

Alicia stormed out of the car, went back to her bedroom, and closed the door. She had not cried since her father had died when she was five, and now she was crying for the second time in three days. But nobody would see her cry this time. She collected herself quickly. She was not sure what she was going to do, but she was not going to share Kanoro's decision with anyone just yet, and she was not going to sit idly while the soldiers searched the forest.

"Let's file all of the camera trap photos and get those cameras back out as soon as we can," she said to Peter.

Chapter 42) A Clue

The helicopter circled and hovered for several hours. The crew knew that their infrared camera could not penetrate a concrete building, but they were surprised to discover that it couldn't get through the forest canopy either. The search of the forest floor would have to be left to the soldiers.

The pilot flew the helicopter in wide circles over the fields that bordered the forest, scattering a few farmers and a family of servals that were hunting mice at the tree line. The infrared camera picked up lots of bright white images of warm, munching cows.

The pilots then decided to fly over the beds of the Gumba and Pfunda rivers. The broken canopy over the watercourses allowed them to see the ground. The pilot descended to 1,000 feet and decreased airspeed to get good looks. The flight engineer used the color camera first. He saw soldiers crossing the water at several points, sticking rigorously to the search grid. They hovered over the Kazaneza Falls, admiring its beauty. It took all of Rain's courage to sit, hidden, just inside the cave entrance, blocking Elizabeth from signaling to her rescuers.

Overnight rains had swollen the waterfall into a raging, roaring torrent. Two soldiers arrived at the base of the falls at mid-morning. They scanned the rock face, but, like countless others, dismissed the many fissures as superficial. They did probe the area behind the falls with a long branch, and were satisfied that there was no cave beneath the sheet of water. The soldiers moved on, doggedly following their transect line directly up the steep hillside on the other side of the river. Elizabeth was unaware that they had been there. The sounds of the water and the helicopter were deafening.

The flight engineer switched from video to infrared and asked the pilots to fly up and down the rivers again. They began by flying downstream. The cold waters of the rivers glowed black on the flight engineer's video screen. The surrounding shorelines and the few small open fields through which the rivers meandered at lower, flat elevations appeared in varying shades of gray. There! A few spots of white. He switched to color video and zoomed in, the crew straining for a visual ID. The white images were three large crowned cranes.

The pilots reversed course and flew upstream. This time, the flight engineer could train the helicopter's infrared camera on the face of the falls. The main torrent was deep black, as were the many small rivulets that flowed down the rock face to the left and right. The cool now-dry stones were dark gray.

"Go back, give me another flyover of the falls!" the flight engineer radioed to the pilots. "As low and slow as you can."

"I've got a hot spot near the top of rock face, to the right of the falls. And one of those little streams down the face is warm. What can you see?"

"Let's go around again," said the co-pilot.

On this pass, the engineer switched to color video and

zoomed in on what appeared to be a deep fissure in the rock. It was a bit discolored at the bottom, as if it had been scuffled or disturbed, but there was no sign of life.

"Nothing", the three agreed. "One more time?"

"Let's get ground personnel to rappel down the face and check out that fissure."

"I found something," came the voice of a soldier over their cockpit radio. The soldier gave his GPS coordinates. The pilot banked the helicopter around and headed downriver. They could see a circle of several soldiers standing above the riverbank, staring at something on the ground. The flight engineer zoomed in with the camera. The object was a machete.

All thoughts of the fissure now forgotten, the flight engineer slid open the side door of the helicopter and lowered a cable with a mesh bag on the end. The pilots hovered, the soldiers caught the bag, and put the machete inside. The engineer retrieved the bag, shut the door, and the pilots zoomed off to the schoolyard.

"We're low on fuel and time anyway," one pilot said to the other. "We need to refuel in Goma and get back to our Sudanese paradise by dusk."

The heat of Rain's and Elizabeth's bodies continued to radiate from the fissure. Most of the heat came from Rain, who was sitting just inside the entrance of the cave. But the glow of the heat could only be detected on the outside by thermal imaging, and the only thermal imaging device in this part of the world would soon be on its way back to Sudan.

The trickle of Elizabeth's morning urine was cooling rapidly.

Chapter 43) The Machete

"Is this yours?" Habimana asked Alicia. He was questioning her, alone, in a classroom. Peter waited outside.

"Yes," she answered.

"How do you know?" he asked.

"The blade is stamped with 'Tramontina – Made in Brazil'. It's probably the only Brazilian-made machete in Rwanda."

"When did you last see it?" he asked.

"I left it with Elizabeth when she had to go."

"Why?"

"To fill in the hole I dug for her. That's what we do in the forest."

"What did you do while she was... 'going'?"

"I walked back to where Peter and Whitney were waiting, to give Elizabeth some privacy."

"How long before you went to find Elizabeth?"

"I've told you all this before."

"How long?"

"About 15 minutes."

Minister Kanoro walked into the classroom. Habimana deferred to him.

They could hear the returning soldiers gathering on the soccer field and boarding the trucks for the trip back to their barracks.

"I have spoken with the platoon lieutenants," the minister began. "We all agree that Miss Weatherby was kidnapped while she was alone in the woods. A soldier found the machete down the hill, near the river, where there are no trails. Her kidnappers probably took the machete away from her and then dragged her or forced her to walk down the hill. It's a difficult place to cross the river, and they dropped the machete."

"There's no blood on it," observed Habimana.

Kanoro continued: "We all agree that the Weatherby girl is no longer up here. We searched the forest and all of the houses in the immediate area. You could not hide a *mzungu*... uh... a blonde American up here for more than two days without somebody noticing. We'd know by now."

Kanoro recovered quickly from his unministerial use of *"mzungu"*, which Rwandans use to describe white people.

"We are confident that you and Peter and Whitney were not responsible," said the minister. "At least not directly. None of this would have happened if you had not foolishly hosted tourists."

"I think the poachers came back for another ape and saw a chance to take a bigger prize. Your pygmy is involved," said Habimana.

"So where is Elizabeth," asked Alicia, relieved to know that at least she was in the "involved-but-not-responsible" category.

"They took her off the mountain the night she disappeared, before we set up the roadblock. She's probably in Gisenyi or Ruhengiri or Goma," answered Kanoro.

"What now?" asked Alicia.

"*Your* future is clear, at least for the next two weeks," sneered the minister. "The army will be searching for the girl in Rwanda, and we'll try to get some cross-border cooperation to search in the DRC, particularly in Goma."

"We'll hear from the kidnappers soon. They're just hunters. They've never made a ransom demand before. They usually just sell what they kill," said Habimana.

Habimana and Kanoro sat back, their smugness diminished

by the student-sized chairs and desks at which they were sitting. The meeting was clearly over.

"Can I have my machete?"

"No, it's evidence. You won't be needing it anyway," said the minister.

"Have you told Mrs. Weatherby all of this?"

"Yes, she's already headed to Gisenyi to wait to hear from the kidnappers. She took the other girl with her. Her parents want her back home," said Habimana.

"Rwandan army finds scientist's missing machete in Gishwati Forest. Conclude that Elizabeth Weatherby was kidnapped. No ransom demand yet. Search moved to cities," read Whitney's last tweet. She did not have enough characters to add: "Scientist not a suspect." That fact would not come out until the next day's edition of the *Wall Street Journal*.

Alicia's grant manager at the Ark Foundation, now one of Whitney's almost 2,000 followers, put a hold on any further transfers into Alicia's Rwandan bank account and sent Alicia an e-mail: "What is going on there?"

Alicia trudged back to the field station.

"God, it's quiet," said Peter.

"Let's get a drink," said Alicia.

Mama Bernard served a Primus to Alicia and a Fanta to Peter.

"That American lady paid me for all of the food and drinks for the police and the army, and some extra. Your drinks are free tonight. Want something to eat?"

"What now?" Peter asked Alicia. "Can we put the cameras out tomorrow and get back to work? The chimps must be terrified."

"That's a long story," said Alicia, and she began to pass on the minister's bad news.

Chapter 44) Honey

Stone and Ja, and Rain and Elizabeth had heard the helicopter fly off to the north and the heavy trucks begin their torturous descent down the mountain. They had no way of being certain that the search of the forest was over. Elizabeth was not even sure that there had been a search, but her soaring hopes were now ebbing rapidly. Ja was quite sure that he was still a wanted man, and would be as long as the Weatherby girl was missing.

Carrot did not appear at dusk to take over, and Rain was too frightened to even leave the cave to gather fresh leaves for their nests.

Elizabeth opened a power bar, and offered half to Rain. Rain liked it, and whimpered softly to acknowledge the sharing.

"You're welcome," said Elizabeth out loud. *God, I've got to get out of here. I'm starting to talk to the apes. Is this like the whatdotheycallit syndrome, when prisoners become friendly with their captors?*

Rain gained the courage to peek out of the cave as dusk fell. She returned immediately with a waxy gob of a beehive, dripping with honey.

"Where did you get that?" asked Elizabeth. *The Stockholm Syndrome, that's it, the Stockholm Syndrome.*

"That didn't just fall there," said Elizabeth, now speaking out loud to both herself and Rain.

She reverted to thinking: *Somebody, some ape or some person, brought it and left it. A chimpanzee would have come inside. Who is leaving food for me? Why don't they tell Dr. Oliveira or the police where I am?*

Rain gave Elizabeth the whole chunk of beehive. The girl found the honey to be sweet and fruity tasting. Rain licked her fingers and wiped her hand on some leaves.

"Here, take half," said Elizabeth. "You haven't eaten today either."

They licked the wax clean. Elizabeth took a picture of Rain eating honey. The flash startled Rain. Elizabeth showed her the picture.

"It's you," said Elizabeth, pointing to Rain. Rain either did not recognize herself or was unimpressed.

Rain crumbled up some green leaves and used them to sponge up the fresh, cold water that trickled down the cave's walls. She tipped her head back and squeezed water into her mouth. She repeated the routine and handed the sponge to Elizabeth. The girl imitated the ape, becoming a chimpanzee tool user. Elizabeth used some of the water to wash off her hands and lips. Eating honey from a beehive is messy. Now her phone was sticky.

They fell asleep in last night's nests.

Chapter 45) A Message from Stone

Alicia decided at breakfast the next morning that she would stay back at the field station. She had read the "What is going on there?" e-mail from her grant manager and needed to answer. It would be a long, difficult reply.

She also decided that there was no sense in putting the cameras out in the forest for the few days that remained of her study. The follow for the day was Thistle, a juvenile male. Peter did not know where he had nested and was expecting to have to walk across the entire forest to find the frightened apes. He was also planning to identify as many of the chimpanzees as possible and verify that they were OK.

Peter was happy to be back in the forest. He could see where the soldiers had trampled the vegetation but knew that the forest would erase all signs in a week.

Ja materialized out of the forest. Ja startled Peter every time he did this because he did not just appear, he materialized, as if from the morning mist.

"God Ja, stop scaring me," Peter said.

"Are the soldiers coming today?" asked Ja.

"No, I don't think so. They think that Elizabeth was kidnapped and has been taken down to Gisenyi or somewhere," said Peter.

"Good. Very scared yesterday. Hard to hide," said Ja.

"It's good that you hid," said Peter. "The police are still looking for you. They think you helped to steal Bee and kidnap Elizabeth."

"Her name is Elizabeth?" asked Ja. "That is hard to say"

"Try Lizbeth. Everybody will know who you mean."

"Why did the police and the soldiers stop looking for Lizbeth?" asked Ja.

"They found Dr. Alicia's machete in the forest, and that made them believe she was kidnapped."

"I found it first," said Ja, "But I was afraid to take it."

"Good decision. What do you think happened to her?" asked Peter.

"Kidnap, sure," answered Ja.

"Did you help?" asked Peter.

"I saw them with her. I did not take her but I am helping her," said Ja.

"Helping her, how?"

"She is safe. I bring her food."

"You know where she is?" asked Peter, his voice raised a few decibels.

Ja also did not know the concept "plausible denial", but he knew Peter was better off not knowing where Elizabeth was.

"Not say, but I protect her."

"Ja, I have to report this to the police," said Peter.

"Not yet, please," said Ja. "Here, Stone sent this for you."

It was piece of white paper, wrinkled and dirty. Peter unfolded it and saw the photos of Bee and Stone.

"Where did you find this?" asked Peter.

"Stone left it for me this morning. I think he wanted me to take it to you. He is afraid of all the soldiers."

"They could not care less about Stone... " Peter said, his

voice trailing off as the understanding formed in his mind.

"Are you saying that Stone took the girl?" Peter asked, hardly believing what he was saying.

"He took girl for Bee," said Ja.

"Wait, wait. Are you saying he took the girl to punish, uh... to hurt the people who killed Apple and took Bee?"

"No, those bad people not care about a girl," said Ja. "He will give girl when Bee comes back."

Peter's first thoughts were the zoo ape and the popsicle-for-light bulb trade, and the gorilla that traded the little boy for food.

"He's holding the girl for ransom, uh... to trade for Bee?" Peter could usually communicate easily with Ja, but now they were discussing some things about which neither had spoken much in their lives.

"Yes. Must get Bee or no girl."

"But Ja, I have to tell the police."

"Not now. I protect her. Stone protect her," said Ja.

Ja de-materialized, leaving Peter alone, in the forest, with a dilemma that was as big and noisy as the helicopter.

Chapter 46) Peter's Dilemma

Peter sat on a fallen log and tried to absorb what Ja had just told him.

Could the chimpanzees even come up with a plan to take the girl and hold her as ransom for Bee? Did they have the memory and the sense of future to think that through? Peter remembered Alicia's accounts of how zoo apes would trade forbidden stuff like rakes and light bulbs for food. Isn't ransom just a trade? But could they conduct such a transaction over days? He remembered Alicia's telling him that the zoo apes sometimes collected stones from their outdoor yards and kept them all day and carried them inside when they were brought in for the night. That's a future plan. The apes even broke off pieces of concrete to get an endless supply of trading material! This proved that they could envision the future and plan for it. Yes, he concluded, the apes could have come up with the kidnapping plan.

But did they? Ja could be lying, placing responsibility on the apes when it was Ja himself, and maybe his wife and friends, that had kidnapped Elizabeth. They could surely have taken her and hidden her up here for a few days. Ja could have kept Peter's picture-message the whole time. Stone may never have seen it. But why? Money? Did they plan to buy new shoes or tin roofs for their huts? Hardly. They had little use for money and would arouse suspicion if they had more than a few cents to spend at any one time.

Maybe the Batwa did it to get Bee back, and restore some of the fabric of their Gishwati home. No. For all of the injustice that they had suffered over the last years, they were generally law-abiding. Their strategy was to stay in the shadows and cope.

Peter concluded that it actually made no difference if Ja or Stone kidnapped Elizabeth. Neither would ask for money. The only plausible motive was to get Bee back.

How, Peter wondered, could he inform the authorities that Elizabeth would be found and returned if they returned Bee? Could he say that he "just had a feeling?" No, he was known to be too levelheaded for that to be acceptable. He would be arrested and interrogated. True, he did not know for certain where Elizabeth was being kept, but Clay Cave was a good guess and it would not take much pressure for him to disclose the presence of the cave. He had known of Clay Cave for years, having secretively watched both chimpanzees and Batwa go in and out. Peter could not resolve this. He moved on with his thinking.

How could they even find Bee? A week had passed and there had been no sign of her. Not a clue. Stone's world was Gishwati and the occasional glimpses of Lake Kivu below that he could get on cloudless days. In Stone's small world, it was obvious that Bee was close and could easily be found by well-intentioned people. But Peter knew that Bee might be dead by now or even be in a sheik's private zoo in Qatar.

Should he tell Alicia? Could she convince Habimana and Kanoro that Elizabeth would be returned if Bee were found? No, same problem for her. Better to keep her out of it. He had, after all, withheld the existence of the cave from her out of respect for the Batwa's privacy, even though the cave held a key to chimpanzee nutrition. She had always wondered why small mineral crystals were sometimes present in the chimpanzees' feces.

Peter was a Christian. He respected the rule of law and he had been raised to know right from wrong. Kidnapping was wrong, illegal. It deprived a person of their right to live freely. But Bee was kidnapped too. Didn't she have a right to live freely? Habimana had already said that apes could be stolen but not kidnapped. Peter thought his pastor would agree. Peter concluded that the life of this girl was more important than Bee's. Beside, two wrongs do not make a right.

Peter also had to think of his own future. He was now unquestionably involved in a girl's kidnapping. At what point would that become responsibility? Legally and morally? He could never forgive himself if something happened to the girl. And he could spend his life in prison if the police found out that he knew where she was.

He made up his mind. As much as he had fought for the survival of the Gishwati chimpanzees, and as committed as he was to improvement in the lives of the Batwa, he would call Habimana this afternoon and tell him what he knew. There would surely be chimpanzee and Batwa casualties when the girl was rescued. The police and the military would be infuriated when they discovered that they had been outsmarted by pygmies and apes.

Ja had assured him that Elizabeth was OK for now. There was no hurry. He would check on the chimpanzees and find

Thistle first. He'd avoid Kazaneza Falls.

Chapter 47) Finding Bee

Alicia was still trying to compose the answer to the "What is going on there?" e-mail at 3 p.m. She was trying to explain the research visa, the tourists, the machete, Whitney's tweets, Elizabeth's disappearance, Apple's killing, Bee's kidnapping, and Kanoro's decision, all without sounding too defensive. It wasn't going well. She was thinking it might be better to call, when her phone rang. Her caller ID said "Habi."

"Hello, Lieutenant. Have you found Elizabeth?" She tried to sound upbeat.

"No, but we've found your monkey."

"*Meu Deus!*" Alicia gasped, lapsing reflexively into her native Portuguese. "Where?" she asked. "By the way, Bee is an ape, not a monkey. Apes are bigger and smarter than monkeys. Sorry, just the scientist in me," she said, already regretting the ungrateful digression.

"Ape, monkey, whatever," he answered. "Goma airport, bound for China via Entebbe and Dubai."

"Is she OK?"

"I don't know. She's in a box with another animal, and they can't get a good look at her."

"What other animal?"

"I don't know."

"I'll drive down right now. I'll meet you at the border crossing."

"I'm not down there," he said. "The RDF in Gisenyi is handling it. The lieutenant there knew I'd be interested."

Habimana explained that a freight handler had intercepted the box in the Goma airport in the Democratic Republic of Congo as it was being loaded on a charter flight to Entebbe, Uganda. The freight handler said that he thought there was a baby in the box, crying. The DRC national police were notified.

The DRC police knew that the Rwandan Defence Force was looking for a kidnapped girl. They peered between the boards into the box, and saw only animals. Illegal wildlife shipments were common at the Goma airport, but the DRC government had recently ordered its military to crack down. One policeman recalled hearing that a baby chimpanzee had been poached recently in Rwanda, and told his commanding officer about the animals in the box. The superior had in turn called the RDF. The shipment was confiscated.

"Who can I talk to in Goma?" Alicia asked Habimana.

"Do you have a visa to enter the DRC?" Habimana responded.

"Damn, no."

"Then you'll either have to try to get one at the border, which will be expensive, or you can wait in Gisenyi," he suggested.

"Why wait? Why can't I just pick Bee up?"

"DRC will have to issue an export permit, and Rwanda will have to issue an import permit."

"Right," said Alicia. "Doesn't the international animal trade law say that the import permit has to come first?"

"That I don't know," said Habimana. "You'll have to call the folks in Kigali."

"Can't we just bring her back, without the red tape?" asked a frustrated Alicia. "Before she dies in that box."

"You know how a policeman has to answer that question," said Habimana. "Do you have any cash around?"

"How much would it take?"

"Ask at the border." He also gave her the phone number of the RDF lieutenant in Gisenyi.

"Thanks," she said. "Anything about Elizabeth?"

"Nothing. No ransom demand yet. Have you heard anything?"

"Nothing here," she answered.

Alicia hung up and collected her thoughts.

She called Dr. Ramona at Gorilla Doctors in Ruhengiri. "We think we found our infant chimpanzee."

"Great, is she OK?" asked the vet.

"Don't know. She's at the Goma airport. I've got to get permits to get her back into Rwanda."

"You won't need to. We have a blanket permit," said Ramona. "We often bring rescued gorillas back here from DRC. I'll meet you in Gisenyi at 7."

"Wonderful. I'll meet you at the border crossing at 7. My assistant will be with me," said Alicia. "Oh, and by the way, they say there's another animal in the crate with Bee."

"Another ape?"

"No idea."

"This should be fun. Hey, what's with the missing girl?"

"Long story," said Alicia, who did not yet know just how long the story would prove to be. "I'll fill you in tonight."

Chapter 48) Bee's Return. Cat Too

Peter walked slowly into the field station at 4 p.m.,

uncharacteristically stoop-shouldered. He was dreading the phone call he had to make to Lieutenant Habimana.

"Why did you radio me to come back early? I don't even know where Thistle and the others will make their nests."

"We have to go to Gisenyi," said Alicia.

"For food?"

"To pick up Bee."

Peter's spirits soared as Alicia told him the story. Stone's (or Ja's) plan just might work yet.

"How much cash do you have? We may need to pay some uh... fees to bring Bee back."

They scraped together 219 U.S. dollars. All "fees" have to be paid in U.S. dollars.

Peter decided on the drive down to Gisenyi that he would not yet tell Alicia what he had learned from Ja today. She had enough on her mind, and she did not need to know the whole story, at least not yet.

"Let me do the talking," said Dr. Ramona, as they met at the border. "Peter, stay here with your car. I'll take Alicia in mine."

Dr. Ramona was no stranger to the Rwandan and the DRC border crossing guards. Her van had "Gorilla Doctors" logos, and she and her organization's work were highly regarded. She explained their mission. Alicia had to pay $150 to buy a visa to enter DRC on her Brazilian passport.

They pulled up at the freight terminal of the Goma airport. There were few scheduled flights in and out of this airport anymore, but the U.N. used it as a base for their humanitarian efforts for refugees in the eastern DRC. U.N. helicopters and planes took off and landed in a steady stream. The airport had just the right mix of bustle and privacy to cover shipments of arms, conflict diamonds, rare minerals, exotic birds, and bushmeat.

They were shown to the crate, which had been set off to the side in the dim, shabby cargo hall. The two women bent and twisted to shine their flashlights through the little crack in the box and look inside.

"Definitely a baby chimp, eyes are open ..," said Ramona, "... and there's a chain around its neck."

"*Merde*," cursed Alicia. "The other one's a serval!"

"Amazing they haven't killed each other. Let's get them out of here," said Ramona. She was already mentally selecting the drugs and dosages she would use to sedate the two different species when they got back to the clinic in Ruhengiri.

"Can't we open the crate here?" asked Alicia.

"I don't want to be chasing animals around this airport," said the vet.

The two women tried to pick the box up but it had no handles. They looked for help to the freight handler and the few policemen that were standing around. The onlookers stood where they were and returned expectant looks.

"Looks like they want some money. You have any?" asked Alicia.

"We don't pay bribes."

Alicia pulled two large bags of Garoto chocolate bonbons, the best to be had in Brazil, from her pack. She gave a lieutenant one bag and gestured that the soldiers and the freight handler should share the other. The lieutenant smiled and waved his hand. The policemen carried the crate gently to the van.

"Got another bag of those for me?" asked Ramona, as they sped back toward the border.

Chapter 49) The Pick-up

Peter had a chance to chat with the Rwandan customs agents and border guards while he waited for Ramona and Alicia. It was dark now, and the steady stream of people coming and going between the two countries had slowed. The border staff was relaxing.

"We're bringing back some animals," Peter said. "Will there be a problem?"

"No problem," said the only agent who even seemed

interested.

"Have you been working here all afternoon?" asked Peter.

"Yup"

"See anything strange or unusual cross into DRC today?"

"It's all strange."

"I mean some sort of medium-sized crate or box bound for the airport."

"Lots of boxes and crates go through."

"This may have been just a single box in a van or truck, or even a car or bus."

The second agent looked up from his phone: "Yeah, about 2. A blue pick-up. Rwandan plates. One wooden box in the back. Seemed odd to be carrying only one box."

"Did you check it?" asked Peter excitedly.

"The driver said it was 'spare engine parts'," said the second agent.

"That's usually code for guns and ammo for the militias," said the first. "We don't check those. Remember, the militias don't officially exist."

"Did you get a signature or the license number or anything?"

"Are you kidding?"

Ramona and Alicia passed back through both sets of customs with no delay. Alicia gave Peter a thumbs up as they passed and headed for the clinic. Peter followed, driving Alicia's Land Rover. As improbable as a sighting would be, Peter found himself to be looking out for a blue pickup truck as they passed through Gisenyi.

Chapter 50) Out of the Box

They arrived at the Gorilla Doctors clinic in Ruhengiri at 11 p.m. Evangeline and John, Ramona's veterinary technicians, were waiting.

They carried the crate into a nearly-empty storage room and closed the door and windows. They all put on gloves and masks.

Ramona prepared two syringes, one with a drug to anesthetize a 30-pound chimpanzee and another for a 25-pound serval. She handed Evangeline the serval syringe.

"I'll keep the chimp syringe, you keep that one. Don't want to mix them up."

Ramona had plenty of experience with wild cats and apes but was not used to sedating two different species at the same time.

The stench from the box was nauseating.

"Let's pry off one board at a time. If an arm or leg comes out, grab it."

The door to the box had been nailed shut and the nails were already rusted. John had to use a hammer and screwdriver to loosen the first board.

Bee sat still, in part from terror and in part from weakness. The cat lay on her lap.

"That's Bee," said Peter. "I can see the mark on her face. God, she's got a chain around her neck."

"Cat syringe!" said Ramona. She reached through the crack and stuck the serval squarely in the hip. "Hold the board back on!" Evangeline checked her watch: 11:17.

"John, put on that big leather glove. Grab Bee's chain when I tell you," directed Ramona.

Evangeline looked up from her watch: "11:22, the cat should be down."

"OK, John, take the board off, and grab the end of the chain."

When the board was removed, Ramona reached into the crate and slapped the cat on the head. No response.

Bee flinched but John had a good grip on the chain. Ramona stuck her with the syringe in an arm.

"11:24," said Evangeline.

"Let's wait a few minutes and take another board off. We should be able to get them out."

Ramona signaled to John, who no longer needed to hold the chain: "When we get the crate open, lay the cat on a blanket on the floor and monitor it. Get a temp, pulse, and a fecal swab. I'll draw some blood when I'm done with the chimp. Let's make up a supplemental in case it starts to wake up."

"11:30."

"Let's get that last board off."

John lifted the serval gently from Bee's lap and laid it on the blanket.

"It's a male," he said.

Alicia and Peter moved Bee to the examination room and laid her on the table. Dr. Ramona and Evangeline went to work.

Chapter 51) Stable Condition

The examinations were completed by 2 a.m. Bee and Cat were each waking up on warm, clean blankets in spanking clean plastic dog carriers. Both animals had been bathed, given some IV fluids, and precautionary antibiotics. Dr. Ramona had removed the shotgun pellets from Bee's fingers and cleaned the wounds. She had also cleaned the cuts caused to the serval's leg by the snare.

John had taken the wooden crate outside and scrubbed it with surgical disinfectant.

"How long has Bee been missing?" asked Ramona.

"Six days," answered Alicia.

"She's in amazingly good shape. Dehydrated and skinny. Was she still nursing?"

"Yes, but she was eating some solid food too."

"Her mother's dead, right? What am I saying? I posted her right here last week. Found some interesting stuff too, but that's for later."

Ramona continued: "We've got to get her fattened up on solids and we'll give her some infant formula. I think I got all of the shotgun pellets out of her hand. Her fingers seem to work fine. We'll keep her on antibiotics."

Peter asked: "Can we put her back with the group?"

"Not right away," said Ramona. "She needs to heal and get her strength back first, and we have to figure out how to return her. These reintroductions don't always go well. We've got some gorilla experience but none with chimps."

"I've got some contacts. I'll check into the reintroduction part," said Alicia.

"The chain," said Peter.

"I'll ask the army to bring some bolt cutters in the morning. Their barracks are right down the road," said Ramona.

"We also have to wait for the blood results. The fecal swabs from the cat and Bee both showed some hookworms, and you saw the lice and louse eggs on their skin. I've given them a dewormer. It should take care of the endos and the lice. We have to be really careful working around them and we have to scrub our hands."

"Technically, we should quarantine them for a month," Ramona continued. "But the sooner we can return Bee, the better. We'll have to take some risk of introducing a disease that they picked up in the past six days when we turn them loose in the forest. The results could be disastrous. A bug that we miss could kill all of those 20 chimps in a heartbeat."

"Do we need permission from Kigali?" asked Alicia.

"Best to at least inform them. Who's your contact, Kanoro?"

"That's another reason we have to hurry this. Kanoro has shut my project down. I have to be gone in two weeks... uh, 12 days."

"Why?"

"He's never liked me, but now he's got me on a couple of procedural technicalities because of the missing girl," said Alicia.

"That sucks. Tell me about the girl," asked Ramona.

"Dr. Alicia – " Peter interrupted, "are we going to go back to Gishwati tonight or staying here?"

"Sleep here, please," said Ramona. "There's plenty of beds and we need to do some planning tomorrow. I have to wait for those two to wake up. Do you have any more of those chocolates?"

"If you don't mind, I'm going to sleep," said Peter, happy to have the credible excuse of fatigue for avoiding the conversation about Elizabeth.

Bee's howl bounced off the finished clay walls. The vet team rushed to the darkened holding room where she and Cat had been sleeping it off.

Bee was rocking her plastic carrier and screaming. She was frantically scanning the room through the mesh door and the air vents. The chain clattered in the box. Cat yowled too. Bee then quieted and began to whimper and strain to see the other carrier.

"Do you think she wants to know where the cat is? After all, they were in the same crate for God knows how long."

Ramona turned Cat's carrier so that its door faced Bee's. Bee reached her fingers through the mesh of her carrier. Cat purred.

"Now I've seen it all," said Ramona.

Chapter 52) Unchained

Two Rwandan soldiers showed up at the clinic with a pair of long-handled bolt cutters.

"Morning, Doc," one said.

"Morning. Come on in. I've got a chimpanzee with a chain around its neck."

Ramona did not want to sedate Bee again, so soon after she had recovered from last night's exam. They cracked open the door of the plastic crate, and John grabbed the chain.

"Ease her out," said Ramona. "She'll probably make a dash for it. We'll grab her by the shoulders and push her to the floor. Watch that she can't bite you."

Bee's screeching was pitiful. The soldier deftly cut the chain from Bee's neck. John and Evangeline relaxed their hold on Bee just enough for her to squirm out of their grip.

"Now we have a problem," Ramona said.

Bee eyed the group from the top of a tall bookcase that fortunately held nothing breakable.

"I guess I'll have to dart her after all," said Ramona. "Let's all leave and I'll make up a syringe."

They all slipped out of the room. Ramona returned moments later with a syringe attached to the end of a long pole. Bee was on the floor, her hands stuck into the serval's cage. Cat was licking her injured fingers.

Alicia and Peter were looking through a small window in the door to the room.

"OK, what now?" asked Ramona.

"Come on out," said Alicia.

"Bring the chain," added Peter.

"Those two really are friends," said Ramona. "Who would have thought?"

"This one looks different from the others," said one of the soldiers, peering through the window.

"She's a chimpanzee," said Ramona. "You've always confiscated baby gorillas. They're both apes, both live in Rwanda. This one's from Gishwati."

She handed each soldier a few bonbons from last night's bag, and thanked them for the help.

"Can't we just leave them both free in that little storage room?" asked Peter.

"No way to clean it. No way to feed them without risking being bitten," said Ramona. "I'm going have to stick her and put her back in the crate."

"All the more reason to get moving," said Alicia.

You don't know the half of it, thought Peter.

Chapter 53) Unwanted Attention

Mango made his move at dawn, threading his way through the forest to Clay Cave. Rain, as instructed, screamed when he appeared, but Stone and the others were still hiding uncertainly at the far edge of the forest, anticipating the arrival of more police. Mango mounted Rain roughly at the cave's entrance, and then shoved her out of the cave, ignoring Stone's warning to avoid any action that would bring attention to the cave, which was indeed being observed.

Mango swaggered into the cave upright, on two feet, in a human-like way. He confronted Elizabeth.

I know this one, she thought. *He's a male. I didn't like his look from the beginning.*

Mango's penetrating brown dark eyes lacked the empathy of the females that had guarded Elizabeth previously. He had heavy bony ridges over his eyes, where humans had eyebrows, and he emanated an odious power. Mango leered. His huge teeth were deeply stained from 20 years of eating tannic foods. He stared, not in curiosity but in lust. Mango moved to within a few feet of Elizabeth. She began to cry from fear. He grabbed Elizabeth's shoulders and began to lick her tears, leaving a slimy film of chimpanzee spittle on her cheeks.

Mango pressed on. His hands slipped to Elizabeth's hips, and he began to tug at the waistband of her pants.

No, this is not why they took me, thought Elizabeth. *Where are the others?*

Ja had seen Mango's arrival at Kazaneza Falls, and the little man responded swiftly. He put his machete down and crept across the rock face by gripping with calloused feet and hands, like a gecko on a wall. He slid into the cave, and saw Mango's massive body enfolding the helpless girl.

Ja leapt on Mango's shoulders and bit him on the neck. Mango screamed and turned violently, thrashing at the attacker that clung to his back. He swung a hugely muscled arm and threw Ja to the floor of the cave. Ja tried to break his fall with an outstretched arm but he was thrown with such force that his wrist snapped and his head hit the rock wall. He was unconscious. Blood began to flow from the cut. Rain was outside, screaming her head off.

Ja's attack deterred Mango. The ape was momentarily confused and, staring at Ja's inert, bloody body, suddenly realized the enormity of his offense. He had violated the culture of his group, which included millennia of peace and trust between chimpanzees and Batwa in the Gishwati Forest. He now sensed that he had violated Stone's plan. He knew he would be exiled, and decided to get a head start to avoid the mortal wounds that would be inflicted if he were caught by Stone and the other males.

Chapter 54) The Plan

Alicia called Lieutenant Habimana at the same time as Mango was making his getaway to nowhere.

She told him that they had recovered Bee and a serval cat and that both were safely in Ruhengiri and in pretty good condition. They would return both animals to the forest as soon as they were stable and found to be disease-free.

"Thank you for helping to get Bee back," she said. "You never really gave up."

"I'm more worried about the girl. There's still no sign of her," said Habimana.

"The Rwandan border guards told Peter that Bee may have been driven into DRC in a blue pick-up," reported Alicia. "Interesting coincidence. At one time you were thinking that Bee's and Elizabeth's disappearances might be connected, and we're pretty sure that a blue pick-up was in Kinihira the night Bee was taken."

"That is interesting," Habimana said. "Worth following up. I'll call the police in Gisenyi and Goma. You'll make a cop yet."

"Good, I need a job," Alicia said.

"I heard," he said. "Did you call Kanoro about the monkey?"

"Bee's an... Never mind. No, I'll call him now."

Minister Kanoro was not available to take her call. Alicia asked his secretary to tell him that they had recovered Bee and that they would soon be putting her back with her group in the forest.

Alicia asked Peter to take a motorcycle taxi back to Gishwati and check on the chimpanzees.

"I'm going to stay here to help Dr. Ramona with Bee," said Alicia. "I also need to start brushing up on ape reintroductions. Better internet and phone connections down here."

Peter put Bee's chain in Alicia's Land Rover and caught a moto taxi for the agonizing three-hour trip up the mountain.

Alicia learned that there were approximately 750 orphaned chimpanzees and gorillas in Africa. In most cases, their mothers had been shot for bushmeat. Ape infants are instinctively driven to cling to their mothers, even when the mother is dead. The hunters find the baby on the body and think they can make a few extra dollars selling it as a pet. Sometimes the hunters get caught and the police confiscate the infants.

The police don't know what to do with these orphans. Most African countries don't have zoos. Over the years, caring people and organizations, mostly American and European, have started "orphanages" or "sanctuaries", where these baby apes are nursed back to health and put back in the company of others, and many are able to live in big, fenced pens or on islands in the forest. The ultimate goal is reintroduction to the wild, but most of these orphans are too damaged for that. Also, wild chimpanzees and gorillas do not readily accept strangers.

But there have been some reintroductions. By searching the Internet, reviewing the records in the Fossey Fund's Ruhengiri library, and calling scientists in other parts of Africa, Alicia was able to find accounts of twenty chimpanzee and gorilla reintroductions. She built a database.

At supper, wearing a clean set of borrowed clothes, Alicia was able to brief Ramona.

"The bad news is that most of these didn't work, but the good news is that a few did.
The key issues seem to be the baby's age, whether it's weaned or not, and whether the field team knows what group it was poached from," said Alicia.

"Assuming, of course, that the baby is healthy?" asked Ramona.

"Yes, to the degree that they can tell," said Alicia. "They don't always have all of the critical health information. They often don't have time to run all of the tests, and the vet support is not always there."

Alicia reddened when she realized what she had said: "Thank God we have the vet support. But we don't have much time."

"So tell me more about the reintroductions," asked Ramona,

taking no offense.

"Well, first, everybody agrees that little apes, up to about three, need to have social contact. Otherwise they get depressed and go downhill. Most of these poor guys are traumatized. They saw their mothers get killed. They need some love and cuddling."

"How do they give them contact?" asked Ramona.

"Human foster mothers."

"Sounds risky."

"It can be at first. The babies may bite and resist the approach. But they usually come around fast. Their need for contact is too strong," said Alicia.

"So you're going to become a mom?" Ramona kidded.

"Somebody has to. I'll try," said Alicia, not at all kidding.

"We've been giving her some formula from a bottle today, but Evangeline sticks it through the mesh," said Ramona.

"I want to give it a try with the crate door open," said Alicia.

"Well, she didn't attack me when I went in there this morning to get her back in the crate after we cut off the chain. She went in by herself to get some bananas. I didn't have to sedate her," said Ramona. "OK, we'll give it a try this evening if you want. What else did you find out?"

Alicia reported: "The chimpanzees and gorillas in most of these reintroductions were released as groups. The apes knew each other, and most were older than three. Some of these were actually born in captivity, but that's another story. We need a plan right now, not a story."

Alicia continued: "The group reintroductions don't really apply to Bee's case. But I found accounts of five orphaned gorillas being reintroduced alone. All were between one and three years old. In at least three of these cases, the youngster was returned to a group that was not its own. All three got roughed up severely by the other gorillas at first. Two had to be rescued and returned to the orphanage. One finally stuck to a group but died a year later. The other two babies were reintroduced to their own groups. They were picked up by older gorillas and never seen again. Who knows what happened to them. In one of these cases, the big silverback male of the group charged the person that brought the baby to the forest. Very dangerous. Good lesson there."

"I knew about the gorillas," said Ramona. "Not exactly encouraging. What about chimps?"

Alicia continued: "One five year-old chimpanzee was reintroduced alone in Uganda but probably not to her own group. She interacted with other chimpanzees but never totally readjusted to life in the wild. Another, in Senegal, was nine months old, a female. This is the most similar to Bee's case. I talked to the scientist that did the reintroduction today."

"The baby's group had been attacked by dogs, hunters'

dogs," Alicia continued. "The dogs caught the baby's mother and ripped her up pretty badly. She survived, but the baby got knocked off her during the attack. The hunters grabbed the baby before the dogs got to her. The baby was confiscated from the hunters just two days later. She was only nine months old and obviously still nursing, probably eating very little solid food. Bee is 19 months old and is eating some solids. The researchers knew who the baby's mother was and they could find the group. Of course, Bee's mother is dead but we can find her group."

Ramona leaned forward: "So what happened?"

"The field team kept the baby for only three days, just to make sure it was healthy. Then they carried the baby to the group in a burlap sack so the apes wouldn't get excited and attack the people while they still had the baby. Like I said, this is a real danger. They put the sack on the ground, opened it, and retreated. A young male came down out of a tree and the baby climbed on to him. The male went back up the tree, and the mother came over to him. Baby climbed on mom, nursed. The baby lived for at least four more years and then was no longer seen with the group."

"It's just one case but it shows it can be done," said Ramona.

"Do we have a plan?" asked Alicia.

"Done. Now get in there and feed your baby."

Chapter 55) Nursing

Elizabeth was dabbing Ja's head wound with a sponge of wet newspaper when Stone, alerted by Rain's screams, burst through the cave entrance. His eyes darted from Elizabeth to Ja and back. Rain stood behind him, whimpering. Stone turned and embraced her. Rain had now been forgiven for letting Mango get in. Stone remembered how Mango had stared at Elizabeth and suspected that it had been Mango who had now threatened the girl so severely that she still wept. Stone was also sure that it was Mango who had struck Ja with an obviously forceful blow. Both were capital offenses in Stone's eyes. He wanted to comfort Elizabeth but did not know how. Maybe Rain could, he thought, but now he had to hunt, and not for a monkey.

Elizabeth looked at him and sobbed. "You have to let me get help for him."

Stone did not understand the words but he knew what she meant. He nudged Rain toward Elizabeth and Ja, indicating that she should keep the girl in the cave and help her and Ja if she could. Then he turned and left.

Ja was still unconscious. Elizabeth rolled Ja on to his back and dabbed at his head wound. The bleeding had stopped. His wrist was swelling rapidly and hung at an odd angle, clearly broken.

Elizabeth had not seen many broken limbs during her college sports career but she had seen a good share of severe sprains. Swelling was always an issue, and trainers usually applied ice packs. There was plenty of cold water running down the sides of the cave. Elizabeth soaked the now-bloody newspaper and wrapped it around his wrist. She took stock of what she had in her vest: a few band-aids, a rolled elastic compression bandage that she carried in case she sprained an ankle, a tube of antiseptic cream, and two small two-packs of aspirin. She decided to try to make a splint. She put some antiseptic cream on Ja's head wound.

Elizabeth rummaged through the branches of her nest, looking for some branches of the right length and width to make a splint. She found a sturdy branch and tried to break a piece off. It was too green. She propped the branch on an angle against the cave wall and stepped on it. It bent but did not break. She stomped on it. Nothing. She jumped on it with two feet, and almost fell herself. Nothing. Ja's machete lay useless outside where he had left it to free his hands to crawl across the rocks.

Rain watched all of this intently. She reached over, took the branch, and broke off the leafy end.

Elizabeth was amazed. The branch was still too long. She still needed to break off two right-sized pieces. She propped it against the cave wall and stomped. Rain took the branch and snapped off the correct length.

"One more," said Elizabeth. Of course, Rain did not understand. Elizabeth propped and stomped again. Rain now knew what Elizabeth wanted, and she obliged. Elizabeth now had two sticks, each approximately a foot long and two inches in diameter.

Elizabeth picked up Ja's feet and swung them toward her nest. She picked up his skinny shoulders and moved them closer to the nest. Then the feet again, this time into the nest. Once again, Rain figured out what Elizabeth was trying to do. The ape stood, grabbed Ja by the hands, and lifted his upper body into the nest. Ja was jolted into consciousness and screamed in pain. Rain had not only got him into the nest but had also straightened his wrist, though that was clearly unintended.

Ja was in pain. His eyes flicked at Elizabeth and Rain and surveyed the familiar interior of Clay Cave. Elizabeth held up his head and gave him some water.

"Lay back now," she said. "I'm going to put a splint on your wrist."

"Mango?" he asked.

"I don't have anything to eat now. Let's fix your wrist first."

Elizabeth aligned the two sticks, one on top and one on the bottom of Ja's wrist. She began to wrap the compression bandage around the splinted wrist.

Not too tight, not too loose, she thought, remembering the trainer's words. *Have to keep it stable but also have to allow for more swelling.*

She wet the bandage with cold water when she was done, and showed Ja two aspirin tablets. "Medicine," she said. "For the pain."

"Not medicine," he said. "Need .... leaves." He said something between "need" and "leaves" that Elizabeth could not understand, but she assumed he was referring to a specific kind of leaves.

"I don't have leaves. Take this now," she ordered, surprising herself with her own firmness.

Ja lifted his head and swallowed the two tablets with water. He managed a crooked little smile.

"You OK, Lizbeth?" he asked.

"Me? Yeah, I'm OK but we need to get out of here," she said. *How does he know my name?*

"Mango not hurt you?"

Elizabeth assumed that he was babbling, at the edge of consciousness. How could a mango hurt her?

Elizabeth sat back, taking a break. She tried to smooth out the wet and bloody newspaper. She had passed a lot of time in the past two days trying to learn a few Kinyarwanda words by deducing their meaning from the photos in the paper. She had six written in her little notebook that she was pretty sure she had translated correctly.

Rain was gone.

Where did she go? thought Elizabeth. She moved quickly to the mouth of the cave and tried her phone. Nothing.

She squatted and relieved herself, and squinted in the unaccustomed sunlight. The falls reminded her of a shower.

Oh what I wouldn't do for a warm shower and a toothbrush, she thought.

A great rustling and shaking of branches to her left signaled the arrival of an ape.

Oh God, I hope it's not that nasty one, she thought.

It turned out to be three. Rain, Carrot, and Thistle all poked themselves into the cave.

Elizabeth recognized the two females. The other had conspicuous male parts. He was new.

Rain had two small handfuls of leaves and a root that looked like a pulled-up dandelion. Carrot had an avocado. Thistle had an armload of fresh leafy branches for their nests.

Rain handed Ja the leaves. She cleaned the dirt off the root and gave him that too.

"Ah, ... leaves," he said, with that unintelligible word in between again. Ja immediately shoved several into his mouth and began chewing them with rapid and exaggerated bites. He swallowed them quickly and asked for some water. Elizabeth made a leaf sponge from a handful of fresh leaves that she pulled from the branches, soaked up some water, and squeezed it into his mouth. Rain thoughtfully stashed the rest of the medicinal leaves near Ja's hand. Ja took a healthy bite of the root and chewed and swallowed it with a grimace.

"Forest pain medicine," Ja told Elizabeth.

Chimpanzees and Batwa have learned over centuries that many plants in the forest had medicinal properties. Some kinds helped to cure diarrhea or fevers. Some stimulated childbirth. Some alleviated pain and swelling. The same plant types worked the same ways on both people and apes.

"These chimpanzees seem to know exactly what we need," Elizabeth said to Ja. "It's amazing."

Elizabeth cut open the avocado with her little knife and shared pieces with the three chimpanzees. Ja declined.

"But we have to get out of here, get you some help. Why are they keeping me here?" she asked Ja.

"Maybe they need you," he said.

Rain and Thistle took off, leaving Carrot with the two people in Clay Cave.

Chapter 56) Another Message to Stone

Leonard had nothing to do. Peter and Alicia were down in Ruhengiri. There was no food to cook and nobody to cook it for. No visitors for whom the gate had to be opened, no tired people who needed coffee or showers, no dirty clothes to wash, although Elizabeth would have loved a change of clothes right about then. He found a children's book about monkeys in Alicia's office, the gift of a previous visitor. It was written in simple English, with lots of colorful pictures. He carried a wooden chair out to the street, where he could sit in the sun and see what was going on in Kinihira. He cracked the book and started a self-taught English lesson. First two, then five, soon twenty children crowded around Leonard and his book. Everybody wanted to see, to read. They stood on tiptoes and craned their necks, but there was no shoving for position. Leonard finally invited the kids to come into the field station's little yard and sit down on the grass. He held the book up, and said "monkey", pointing to a picture of a baboon. "Monkey," repeated the kids, giggling and squirming. A new tradition, Leonard's Village Reading Circle, had been born. The student had become a teacher.

The spell was broken by the arrival of Peter's moto taxi at noon. Peter's bones ached from the bouncing ride. The first thing he did was wash his hair. Rwanda has a strictly enforced helmet law for motorcycle drivers and passengers. Moto taxi passengers wear helmets that have been worn by countless others, some with head lice.

It had only been 18 hours since he and Alicia had raced to Goma to get Bee, but it seemed like days. Peter filled Leonard in on Bee's recovery and told him about the serval.

"I'd fix you lunch but we're out of food," said Leonard.

"I got some food on the way up," Peter said. He pulled two tomatoes, two carrots, a thick disk of Gishwati cheese, a loaf of bread, and six hard-boiled eggs out of his pack. "Let's have some lunch, and then I have to head for the forest."

Peter wanted to spend the afternoon looking for all of the chimpanzees and making sure they were OK.

More important though was the Elizabeth-for-Bee swap. Now that Bee had been recovered, there was a real chance that Stone's (and Ja's?) plan could work. He needed to find Ja and make sure that the girl was still alive and well. He needed to find a way to assure Stone that Bee was on her way back. Peter fetched a chisel-pointed red marker from the office before he left.

Once into the forest, Peter noticed that things were different. Stone, Chicken, and Fig passed him overhead in the canopy without even hesitating or looking down at him.

They're on a mission, he thought. *And where's Mango?* The four adult males usually traveled together.

He walked almost to the east side of the forest, and Ja never materialized. Peter found that odd too, and somehow unsettling.

Maybe he took a chance and went home, Peter thought.

Peter walked until dark, following the few chimpanzee vocalizations that he heard during the afternoon. They were quiet today. He visited the bamboo grove and their favorite *umushwati* trees. He finally saw a total of 17. Mango and Carrot were not among them. Peter chose to end his day in the area where Stone had recently been making his night nest. He was about to give up and go home when Stone and some others appeared and hurriedly made their nests. It was too dark to identify all of them. Peter hoped that Mango and Carrot were there.

He reached into his pack and pulled out two more tomatoes, two carrots with their leafy tops, another generous disk of cheese, a loaf of bread, and six hard-boiled eggs, none of which he had shown to Leonard. He wrapped these into a bulky package of newspaper.

Peter then fished the sheet of paper with the pictures of Bee and Stone out of his pack. He sat down and smoothed the paper on his thigh, and used the marker to make one big red circle around both pictures. It was the only way he could think of to signal Stone that he would soon be reunited with Bee. He left the piece of paper on top of the food, and used his mental map to make his way out of the forest in the pitch dark.

Once out of the forest, he called Alicia to report. "I saw everybody but Carrot and Mango. They seem subdued but OK. How are you?"

"Good," said Alicia. "We'll bring Bee back the day after tomorrow if she continues to get her strength back and there are no setbacks. Ramona and I have a strategy for putting Bee back. We'll just need to know where Stone is."

"What's that noise?" asked Peter.

"You wouldn't believe what I'm doing," said Alicia.

Chapter 57) Mommy Time

After supper, Alicia had put on latex gloves and a surgical mask. Evangeline gave her a baby bottle of warm infant formula. She entered the storeroom and sat down on the floor beside Bee's crate. Bee came to the mesh door. Alicia stuck the nipple through the mesh. It was at that moment that Peter had called Alicia. What he had heard in the background was Bee suckling loudly on the bottle.

After the call, Alicia withdrew the nipple and Bee whimpered in protest. Alicia slid open the latch on the crate. Bee and Cat watched this move intently. Alicia opened the door and pushed herself away a few feet. Bee moved hesitantly out of the crate. Alicia showed her the bottle. The baby was ambivalent but her need for comfort prevailed. She moved to within an arm's length of Alicia and began to suckle. Slowly, she began to push Alicia's arm backward and was soon standing on all fours with her shoulder brushing Alicia's. Bee emptied the bottle.

"Now what, little Bee?" said Alicia in her gentlest voice. Bee leaned in to smell Alicia's mouth, and then suddenly wrapped her arms around Alicia's neck. She sat in Alicia's lap and laid her head on the woman's chest with a deep sigh. Ramona and Evangeline watched through the window in the door.

Alicia was frozen, afraid to disturb this oddly comforting connection. Bee fell asleep. Alicia felt a stirring of emotion that was completely foreign to her. She felt warm, soft, relaxed, bonded. Bee's little heart beat slowly, just inches from Alicia's, which was now slowing as well.

Now what? thought Alicia.

She could not bring herself to wake Bee up. She reached over to Cat's crate and grabbed the mesh to take some weight off her back. She could feel the silken thickness of the serval's hair even through her latex glove. The cat had pushed the side of its neck and head against the mesh, burying Alicia's fingers. He moved his head slowly up and down, making Alicia an unintentional scratcher. The cat began to purr.

"Well, you need some cuddling too, I guess," said Alicia. So the trio remained, Bee snoring, Cat rubbing, and Alicia sitting uncomfortably on a concrete floor, playing mother to two orphans. All three were getting some needed cuddling.

Evangeline opened the door after an hour. "That enough," she said," "We don't want the babies to get too dependent on humans."

What about me? thought Alicia. *I could get pretty hooked on this too.*

Evangeline nudged Bee back into the crate and slid the bolt. Alicia stood stiffly. It was 10PM. Bee whimpered. Lights out.

Chapter 58) Madam Chen

Alicia had slept unusually well. She awoke at 6 a.m. and was looking forward to her breakfast, and to Bee's.

Ramona made scrambled hens' eggs and herbal tea.

"You'd better come see this," said John.

He led them to the storeroom. Both crates were open. Bee and Cat were wrestling gently on the floor.

"Didn't you lock her crate?" asked Ramona.

"I slipped the bolt," said Alicia.

"Well, one of them figured out how to slide it out and then freed the other."

"Make up a bottle, John. Alicia has an ape to feed," said Ramona. "We can live with this. It's only one more day. Whatever germs or parasites one has, the other has them anyway."

"Still mask and gloves?" asked Alicia.

"Still mask and gloves," said Ramona. "And get fecals from each. We'll check on those hookworms."

Alicia and John both entered the room. Alicia had Bee's bottle. John had a plate of ground raw meat for the serval, and a bowl of chopped fruits and veggies for Bee. The serval jumped to the top of the bookcase. Bee approached. John put down the food and carefully scraped up samples of the freshest cat and ape feces.

"We'll run these now," he said as he left.

Alicia sat and held out the bottle. Bee came to Alicia's lap and suckled loudly. Alicia noticed that the ape was putting some flesh back on her bones. Cat came down and ate too.

Alicia fished the ringing phone out of her shirt pocket.

"How's the monkey?" Lieutenant Habimana teased.

"The *ape* is doing very well. We plan to release her tomorrow."

"Where are you now?" he asked.

"Ruhengiri, at Gorilla Doctors."

"I need you in Gisenyi."

Habimana told her that the Gisenyi police had found the blue pick-up and arrested the driver. They had found a shotgun, snares, and a net in the truck. Faced with a long stretch in a Rwandan prison, the driver quickly identified his younger accomplice, and together they traded their freedom for implicating Madam Chen. The police had burst into Madam Chen's store at the bus station, disrupting rush hour arrivals and departures.

"Elizabeth was not there and we found no sign of her. Chen may have been tipped off by the search for a blue pick-up. We found some bushmeat, smoked and frozen, in her store. There is an ape hand in her freezer. Didn't your dead chimp have its hands cut off?"

"Yes, but I'm not sure I could identify the frozen hand as

Apple's without a DNA test."

"How long would that take?"

"Weeks, maybe more. We'd have to send samples to Germany."

"Why Germany?"

"No DNA lab yet in Africa, unless you guys have one."

"No, unfortunately, not yet. Anyway, can you come over here? There's some other stuff we'd like you to see."

"OK, give me an hour and a half. I need to do some shopping anyway," said Alicia. "Food and some stuff for tomorrow."

Alicia hung up, left the storage room, and briefed Ramona on the developments in Gisenyi.

Ramona said: "OK, go over there. We've got to get ready for tomorrow. John and I will have to think of everything and get ready for anything."

"Should I come back here or go straight back to Gishwati?" asked Alicia.

"Up to you," said Ramona. "We can bring Bee and the cat up tomorrow."

Parking was usually a chaotic and risky undertaking near the bus station in Gisenyi, but today the police waved Alicia to the curb directly in front of Madam Chen's store.

Madam Chen was sitting sullenly in the back of a police car. Alicia glared at her.

Habimana was in the back room.

"Is that crate like the one that Bee and the cat were in?" he asked.

"Almost exactly."

"Look at this rope. What kind of hairs are those?"

"Could be serval. Can't be sure without DNA."

"Look at these piles. Chimp poop?"

"Could be. Can't be sure without DNA."

He walked to the freezer and took out the hand. "Chimp?"

"Yes, left hand. Adult."

"The mother's?"

"Can't be sure - "

" - without DNA, I know," he interrupted.

"The guys admitted to stealing the chimp, bringing it here, and taking it across the border to the airport. But without real proof, the woman will never be convicted of killing and stealing the apes. Her lawyer will say that they were framing her."

"Well, I wish I could help but I can't lie," said Alicia.

"She'll be free to try again, unless we can find where she took Elizabeth."

"Do you think she's behind Elizabeth's kidnapping?"

"You got a better idea?" he asked. He paused and added: "Sorry, I'm just a little frustrated. She'll get a slap on the hand if all we've got is the bushmeat."

"I'm sorry, Lieutenant. Is there anything else I can do? We've got to get ready to put Bee back in the forest tomorrow."

"Is that easy to do?"

"About a 10% chance of success but we have to try."

"Good luck."

Alicia went out to her Land Rover to get some shopping bags for her trip to the market. Bee's chain and padlock were laying in the back, where Peter had left them.

Lock! she thought.

"Lieutenant, does the woman have keys, like a ring of keys?" she shouted to him as he was briefing his team in the street on the failure of their operation.

A police officer handed him Madam Chen's purse. He dug around inside and withdrew a cluster of keys of all sizes and shapes.

"Here," she said. "This was around Bee's neck."

The lock popped open with the second key.

"If we can't tie her to Elizabeth, this will at least give us grounds to jail or deport her for killing, stealing, and attempting to sell endangered animals."

Madam Chen, her visa revoked, was on a plane bound for Hong Kong two days later. Justice is swift in Rwanda.

Chapter 59) Deeper Bonds

Maybe it was the success of her caring for Ja, or the sweet consideration of her needs by the three chimpanzees, or the avocado, but Elizabeth was adjusting to her life in Clay Cave. She wanted out, to be sure, but she at least felt safe from harm.

She had had the choice of sharing her nest with Ja for the night, or sharing Carrot's nest, or sleeping on the rock floor. Carrot made room for her and they slept together until dawn. Everybody took a short, private wake-up call outside the cave.

Ja was walking but did not go far from the entrance. He

returned with another bundle wrapped in newspaper that he had spotted near the entrance.

The ape, the pygmy, and the American girl sat facing each other on the cave floor as Elizabeth unwrapped the package.

Wow, this one's in English, thought Elizabeth. Peter had thoughtfully wrapped the food in the outer pages of the *Rwandan New Times*, but Elizabeth had no grounds to understand that the choice had been intentional, a sign of Peter's consideration, maybe even a message. At least she would have something to pass the time, although the *New Times* was not known for hard-hitting reporting.

"Tomatoes, carrots, eggs, cheese, bread... a feast," said Elizabeth. She signaled to Ja and Carrot to begin. Both were hesitant. Carrot took a carrot.

"I'm going to call you 'Carrot' from now on," Elizabeth said.

"Carrot, yes, Carrot," said Ja. Elizabeth thought he was *affirming* her choice of a name, but he was *confirming* it. Ja was puzzled about how she could have learned the chimps' names in such a short time. This impressed him and reinforced his commitment to get her out of this safely.

"That's enough. Let's save some," she said after all three had eaten well. She carefully re-wrapped the food and then saw the slashing red letters on the newsprint: "S... O... O... N."

Somebody had sent her a message. *Why don't they just come and rescue me?*

Carrot moved closer to Elizabeth and began to finger the girl's now-grimy hair. The movements of her fingers were soothing, reassuring. Elizabeth held still, barely breathing. She had pulled up her sleeves to wash up, and Carrot shifted her grooming to the silky golden hairs on her forearm. Ja smiled.

"You now," he said, looking at Elizabeth and nodding toward Carrot.

Can I really do this? Elizabeth asked herself. She began to stroke and rub Carrot's forearm. Carrot lay back, her arm in Alicia's lap.

The reverie was broken by a little pink face with elephantine pink ears appearing in the cave entrance. Squash nudged Potato into the cave and came in herself.

Elizabeth smiled broadly and said, to nobody in particular: "Oh my God, is he adorable?" Carrot and Squash embraced. Carrot looked at Elizabeth fondly for three heartbeats, and left. Potato climbed on to Squash, who sat down near the entrance. Elizabeth took out her phone. Power was at 22% but this was too precious to pass up. The flash startled the apes and Ja momentarily, but they had seen flashes before. The shiny pink object in Elizabeth's hand was irresistible to Potato, who climbed off Squash and edged toward Elizabeth. The girl held out the phone. Potato became entranced with his own reflection in the screen, and began to make faces. He reached for the phone but Elizabeth did not turn it over. He somersaulted back to Squash.

Ja wanted to go home, where his wife could tend to his wrist and give him some real food and banana beer, but he was afraid that Mango might return.

"I go now," said Ja to Elizabeth. "Thank you. I will stay near. Mother is Squash. Baby is Potato." With that, Ja left.

S... O... O... N, thought Elizabeth. *How soon?* The date on her phone told her that she had been in the cave for five days.

Chapter 60) Holding the Bag

Alicia walked the two blocks to the sprawling outdoor market in Gisenyi. Tomatoes, potatoes, avocados, cauliflowers, and cabbages were piled in neat cones, like cannonballs. Carrots, cucumbers, leeks, and zucchinis were stacked like cordwood. There were round heaps of beans, flour of various kinds, salt, and sugar, and tiny piles of spices. But Alicia headed first to the stalls from which sheet-sized pieces of brightly colored, boldly patterned cloth were festooned. Tables below were full of teetering piles of folded cloth of the same sort. Alicia began to think about what colors would be best for her work tomorrow.

"Does Madam want a skirt?" asked the proprietress of the stall that had captured Alicia's attention.

"No, a bag," answered Alicia.

"A bag?" the woman said, in a tone that implied disapproval.

"Yes, about this wide," Alicia answered, holding her hands

three feet apart, "And twice as long. Can you make it?"

"Pick your cloth," said the woman. "We have a sewing machine here. Thirty minutes." All of this was communicated by pointing.

Alicia picked a piece of cloth in browns, greens, and slashes of orange, almost camo. She paid for the cloth and went food shopping, thinking more about Bee's meals than her own. She quickly accumulated two heavy bags of fruits and vegetables.

She picked up the sewn bag and crossed to the *boulangerie*, where she bought bread, cheese, sugar cookies, and a cold, outrageously priced can of Coca Cola. She needed some caffeine.

While she was unloading everything into the Land Rover, Alicia saw Augustin drive down Umuganda Avenue in the spotless and shiny Eco-Treks Land Cruiser. Kimberly Weatherby was in the front seat. Lieutenant Martin Habimana had just told her that the morning's promising lead and subsequent raid had failed to provide any evidence of the suspect's involvement in Elizabeth's disappearance or any indication of her daughter's whereabouts. The investigation was at a standstill. Mrs. Weatherby had given up her vigil at the Gisenyi Serena Hotel and was headed back to her apartment in Kigali with a broken heart.

"Very *chic*," said Ramona, fingering the cloth bag that Alicia was showing off at the Gorilla Doctors compound in Ruhengiri. "Why didn't you just get a burlap potato bag?"

"Would *you* like to be carried in a burlap bag?" asked Alicia, perhaps a bit too protectively.

The women laughed, but both were feeling a growing tension about the next day's reintroductions.

"We took Bee off the bottle," said Ramona. "She's going to have to survive on solids from tomorrow on."

Alicia's heart sank in hidden disappointment. She had been looking forward to a feeding and cuddling session with Bee.

"But she still needs the contact," said Evangeline. "Let's cut up some of those goodies you bought and fatten that girl up."

Bee worked her way through her vegetarian buffet and Cat ate his plate of meat. They wrestled and squirmed around and over Alicia, who sat on the floor of the storeroom. Bee finally fell asleep in Alicia's arms. There was no lap room for Cat. He fell asleep jammed against Alicia's leg.

Last time, thought Alicia, a bit wistfully.

Chapter 61) Freeing Cat

They caught Bee and Cat in deep sleep at 4:30 a.m., both in the same crate.

"We need them in separate crates this morning," said Ramona through her surgical mask.

John grabbed the cat by the scruff of the neck and stuffed him quickly into the other crate. The move looked heartless but it was just business. Bee howled in protest.

"Put their breakfasts in the crates, though they probably won't eat on this trip," Ramona told John.

"Can we make some coffee this morning?" asked Alicia. "Your hippy tea won't get me through this day."

Ramona, Alicia, and John ate a simple but large breakfast of toasted bread, jam, and cheese. Evangeline would stay back at the clinic.

"They're as healthy and free of disease as we can get them," Ramona said over breakfast.

John had packed the Gorilla Doctors van with medical field packs and waterproof plastic boxes that held a variety of medical equipment and supplies. They loaded the two animals at 5:30 and headed up the mountain to Gishwati. Peter met them at the field station gate at 8:30 a.m.

"Let's take the serval in first," said Ramona. "Stay here with Bee," she said, nodding to John.

They could hear Bee's wailing until they were deep in the forest. Peter had chosen the flat swampy section along the Gumba River as the serval's release point. The camera trap there had often recorded servals.

Cat became a different animal. His nose twitched at familiar scents. His long ears stood stiffly erect, turning directionally at sounds that only he could hear. He paced intensely in tight circles in the crate. Muscles in his limbs rippled. There was no purring or relaxed rubbing now. Bee seemed to be forgotten.

Peter put down the crate. "I'd like to take some pictures. Would one of you open the crate? Maybe you should both be in the picture."

The women stood on opposite sides of the crate, their masks and gloves looking too clinical for the lush setting.

"Ready?"

"Ready."

Alicia slipped the bolt and opened the door, expecting Cat to shoot out.

Instead, he stuck his head out and looked up and to both sides. He stepped out, spring-loaded.

Peter clicked away. Cat looked back at the women and then strutted off on stiffened legs, majestically, assuredly, into the tall swamp grass.

Cat had been returned to the wild.

"Too bad we didn't have time to get radiocollars for these guys," said Alicia.

"I did tattoo a star on the inside of his right front leg," said Ramona.

Chapter 62) Nuts

Elizabeth Weatherby was reading the *New Times*. She sidled toward the cave entrance to get more of the morning light. She read that heavy rains had caused landslides in Nyabihu District. Several people had been killed and many houses had been destroyed. The article said that the landslides would not have occurred if there had still been forest on the steep slopes above. She did not know where Nyabihu District was, but she thought it had not rained heavily in this area for several days.

Potato was being a pest but continued to be unstoppably cute. Elizabeth's nest was wilted and flattened, and had provided little comfort this night. It needed new leaves. She was also hungry. Squash seemed to be less appreciative of her needs than Carrot and the others had been.

Rain arrived, as if she had been reading Elizabeth's mind. She dropped an armload of leafy boughs and embraced Squash, both squeaking with pleasure. Potato clambered over both and squeezed in between. Elizabeth held out her arm and hand in greeting, in a welcoming combination of a human handshake and chimpanzee touch. She turned her palm up, down, and sideways, trying to get her message right.

Rain opened her groin pouch and pulled out a handful of nuts. They were the size of hazel nuts. She found a rounded stone on the cave floor and began to tap on the nuts, one at a time. The first strike was sharp and forceful, breaking the shell. Then, softer tap, tap, taps to free up but not crush the nutmeat within. She turned the nut between each tap. She ate one nut, gave one to Squash, and one to Elizabeth. Squash took a turn, with Potato watching closely. When she stopped to eat, he struggled to pick up the stone, which he dropped on a nut with no control or precision. The shell cracked but did not open. Squash finished the job. Potato would not become a skilled nutcracker until he was eight or nine, after much practice.

Rain looked at Elizabeth and then at the stone. Elizabeth took the pause to mean that Rain was inviting her to try the hammer. The stone was too big for Elizabeth's hand. She tried it two-handed, and smashed the first nut, inextricably mixing nutmeat and shell. She tried another and caught a little finger beneath the hammer.

"Ouch" she squealed, shaking her hand. Hand-shaking is a gesture of happy excitement for chimpanzees. Rain and Squash joined in Elizabeth's seeming joy. Potato turned somersaults. The few nuts that Elizabeth did get to eat were rich and filling.

Squash picked up Potato and left. Elizabeth allowed herself the luxury of looking at Potato's picture. It made her happy.

Elizabeth, thankfully, would never have to become a skilled nutcracker.

Chapter 63) Freeing Bee

"Well, the cat was easy," said Ramona. "Looks like it's going to rain."

Ramona and Alicia had returned to the field station and were enjoying cups of pressed coffee. Peter had stayed behind and was trying to find Stone.

"Great, as if 10% odds were not low enough, let's throw in a drenching."

"Bee ate her whole breakfast, Dr. Ramona," John reported.

They went over the plan for Bee's release. Peter would radio Stone's location back to Alicia. John would carry Bee in the crate. Alicia and Ramona would carry the medical field packs. Alicia also had the radio and the custom-sewn sack, into which Bee would be transferred when they were close to Stone.

"It's going-home day, little girl," said Alicia to Bee.

Bee wanted out of the crate for some cuddling.

"Sorry girl, but your next cuddle will have to be a chimpanzee cuddle," said Alicia.

"Hopefully," said Ramona.

Peter's voice over the radio startled all four. He gave Stone's location to Alicia.

"He's with Carrot and Thistle and some of the others. I haven't seen Rain, Mango, or Squash and Potato."

"We're on our way. Is Ja there?"

"Haven't seen him for two days. Weird."

The trail had turned muddy and slippery in the pouring rain. John's footing was uncertain. They moved slowly, sweating in their rain gear. Breathing was especially difficult through their surgical masks.

After 15 minutes, they were within 300 yards of the apes.

"Time for the switch," said Alicia. "She's not going to like this much."

John set down the crate. Alicia unfolded the bag and opened the door. Bee came out and embraced her. Ramona slipped the bag over Bee's head and began to inch it down over the rest of her body. She had to be pried off of Alicia. Once in the bag, Bee quickly adjusted and discovered that she could still cling to Alicia through the cloth. Ramona took over the radio.

"OK, we're on our way to you," she transmitted to Peter. "Can you video the release this time?"

"Do my best. This rain will not make it easy," he answered.

Stone threw Alicia an interested glance as she arrived on the path below, with two strangers, an odd poncho around her shoulders, and wearing gloves and a mask.

"I could see the orange in that cloth from a mile away," Peter chattered nervously.

"Are you ready with the video?" asked Ramona. "Stay on Bee as long as you can."

"Let's try to follow them if they take off with Bee," said Alicia. "John, can you take this field kit so I can take some notes later?" John picked up the field kit.

"Everybody ready?"

There were affirmative nods all around. Alicia began to peel Bee out of the sack.

Peter's video would later show that what was to ensue took exactly 55 seconds but it seemed like hours in hindsight.

Thistle was the first to see Bee and quickly descended to the path.

Bee screamed when she saw him. She must have been frightened because she jumped on to Alicia and clung fiercely.

Stone rushed to the ground to rescue his dear baby Bee. His onrushing body knocked Alicia to the ground on her back, but the video would show that he never struck or bit her. His target was Bee. He wrested her off Alicia, who was gasping for breath.

Stone climbed high into a tree, holding Bee awkwardly but firmly. Thistle, Fig, Chicken, Carrot and the others were screaming. It was an unfamiliar screaming, a mix of fear and happy excitement.

Rain, hearing the noise, abandoned Elizabeth in the cave and ran to the scene. Squash and Potato arrived from another direction, Potato hanging on for dear life.

Ja heard the noise but kept his vigil near the cave.

Rain moved toward Stone and Bee and began to groom her little sister.

Joyful whimpering was replacing the screams. It might have all ended happily and successfully right there.

But there was another onlooker. Blinded by his own ambitions, Mango completely misinterpreted the situation.

Chapter 64) Misjudgment

Mango had begun a new, solitary life yesterday morning, after he had attacked Elizabeth and Ja. He would live at the fringe of the forest, in the few spaces that were not occupied by people or chimpanzees. There would be no more bamboo shoots, dewy flowers, monkey meat, and handfuls of sweet fruit that grew inside the dark cool forest. He had instead begun to eat the coarse and bitter leaves of weedy trees, and stolen corn and avocados. He had broken into a farmer's beehive to get honey. He was already beginning to starve. Mango had slept last night in a pitiful nest that he had built in the low shrubbery that grew around a smelly outhouse. Scratches and insect bites festered on his ungroomed skin. He longed to touch and be touched, and listened and watched for any sign of his former friends. He was miserable and desperate. The alternative was certain death at the hands of his former male accomplices or perhaps even from a Batwa spear.

At dawn this morning, Mango had climbed into the crown of a large tree that stood alone at the edge of the schoolyard. He found a few figs to eat, and sat unmoving, watching the forest to the east and the road and Kinihira village to the west. He was hoping to spot an untended baby whose tears he might lick. He had seen an unfamiliar van drive into the field station. Then he saw the scientist woman, Peter, and a stranger carry a crate into the forest. He also saw another crate through the opened door of the van.

Mango did not dare to follow the people with the crate into the forest, opting instead to eat bitter, unripe figs, and wait and watch. After an hour, the people had returned with an empty crate and then took the other crate out of the van. Mango thought that he saw a young chimpanzee inside. He could not restrain himself this time. He had to follow the people as they carried the second crate into the forest.

Mango moved slowly to avoid detection. He was an expert in soundless travel.

His eyes widened when the scientist woman opened the crate. There was indeed a baby chimpanzee inside, and it was Bee!

Mango knew that Stone, Chicken and Fig were close by. He was fearful, but his fear was overcome by an indefinable sense of opportunity, a hope of redemption.

He inched through the trees behind the people as they carried Bee, now covered with a cloth, toward the other chimpanzees. They were bringing Bee back! If only he could get the credit for that.

He lost all sense of place as the people uncovered Bee, as Bee screamed and clung to the scientist, and as Stone rushed down and snatched Bee from her.

Mango would not have the advantage of a slow motion replay of Stone's behavior. He interpreted Stone's actions as an attack on Alicia, perhaps because he himself was a bellicose bully.

But, he reasoned quickly, this was his chance to atone. He would show his great courage and loyalty by *supporting* Stone in the attack on this woman who had taken Bee.

Peter's video camera had been trained on the chimpanzee reunion with Bee that was unfolding rapidly, high in the treetops. He caught the crucial moment when Stone surrendered little Bee to the confident and skilled embrace of her older sister Rain. But he had missed Mango's charge.

So had everybody else. Ramona and John had helped Alicia to her feet after Stone had knocked her over, and they were all peering upward into the canopy when Alicia was hit full bore by 180 pounds of charging chimpanzee.

Mango could have killed her instantly, with a savage bite or a hammer-like blow. But his goal was not to hurt Alicia. His goal was to impress Stone. So Mango did what male chimpanzees do when they want to impress other chimpanzees: a dragging display. In different circumstances, he might have uprooted and dragged a small tree. But now it was Alicia whom he dragged, and he put on a formidable show. He dragged her by the collar of her shirt up the path, running at full speed, hair abristle and hooting loudly. He turned and dragged her by her foot in the opposite direction. He jumped over a fallen log, but Alicia's body did not follow. She was slammed into the log with such force that her foot was ripped out of Mango's grip. He returned and stomped on her now-limp torso with both feet.

Satisfied with his heroism, Mango stopped and looked upward for what he was sure would be his fellows' admiration and approval. This was his second serious misjudgment of the morning.

Chapter 65) Judgment

Stone was neither admiring nor approving. Mango saw him look to Fig and Chicken, and even to Thistle. The four moved toward one another and fell silent, eight eyes fixated on Mango. The hair on their backs and arms was erect. They were scheming. Mango realized his mistake, but it was too late and there was no place to run.

But run he did. Perhaps, he thought, he could escape if he crossed the road.

It was Thistle's first "hunt," and it would turn out to be the most dangerous of his life. But Stone needed male bodies, and it was time to break Thistle in. The juvenile stayed close to Stone. The two of them climbed down to the ground. Fig and Chicken caught up and flanked Mango in the tree canopy as he fled.

A famous Harvard primatologist had written a book about chimpanzees that was titled *Demonic Males*. "Demonic" referred in part to the territorial defense of chimpanzee males, which many find to be brutal and warlike. They were never brutal or warlike to members of their own group, but strange males were attacked and killed. The Gishwati chimpanzees had never experienced an unfamiliar male. The nearest strange chimpanzee male was 50 miles away. But Mango had left the group yesterday and was now an outsider, and Stone's genetic memory kicked in.

Mango ran for his life, already winded by his energetic display. Stone, Fig, Chicken, and Thistle dogged him relentlessly. Mango could not stop to catch his breath. The others could work in relay, one at a time stopping for a short break and then catching up. They stopped screaming to conserve their energy.

Mango stopped, turned, and faced his two pursuers in the branches. Fig moved in from his left. Mango turned toward him. Chicken leapt on his back and bit his ear off. Mango screamed and flung his arm at Chicken. Fig charged in and bit Mango in the thigh, nicking his femoral artery. Small but strong spurts of exertion-pressurized blood began to fountain from Mango. Now his strength would quickly wane.

He began to flee once more. Chicken and Fig overtook him easily and pulled him over backward. Mango lost his footing and fell 40 feet to the ground. Stone and Thistle were waiting below. Chicken spit out Mango's lower lip, and he and Fig headed down. The fall and the blood loss left Mango helpless.

Thistle watched as Stone dug his huge canine teeth savagely into Mango's groin and dismembered him, the ultimate demonic male chimpanzee brutality. Thistle would learn a lot about hunting and about the chimpanzee code of behavior this day.

Now, the males began to scream, embracing and clasping arms and hands. They stomped on Mango's dying body. Mercifully, the rogue was feeling no more pain.

Chapter 66) Alicia

Alicia lay unmoving but she was moaning. She was conscious and feeling pain. Her rain jacket was shredded and one boot had come off. Ramona did a quick emergency assessment: pulse a little slow but strong, breathing OK, pupils responsive and equal, no obvious broken limbs, no deep cuts or cracks in the skull, no serious external bleeding. No life-threatening injuries. Both women heard chimpanzees screaming in the forest during the examination.

Alicia spat out a front tooth. Her face was cut and scratched. Pebbles and bits of bark were embedded in her forehead.

She had a bloody nose. Her hair was dirty and matted.

"Where does it hurt?" asked Ramona.

"Knee, ankle, everyplace," rasped Alicia.

Ramona and John rechecked her ankles and knees. They did not seem to be broken.

"Probably sprained or a torn ligament," Ramona said to John.

"Go get help," Ramona said to Peter. "We need to get her out of here and up to the clinic. There's a stretcher in the van."

Leonard was monitoring a walkie-talkie at the field station as he was going about his chores. Peter radioed him to round up six men, get the stretcher, and meet him at the road on the west side of the forest.

Peter then sprinted through the driving rain to the road. He saw Mango's blood-soaked body on the trail, and stopped briefly to cut a few boughs and cover him. He wanted to spare Alicia's rescuers the gruesome sight.

Three men and three of the strongest women in Kinihira, including Mama Bernard, waited at the trailhead.

"Another chimpanzee hurt?" asked Mama.

"Yes, but so is Dr. Alicia," Peter said. "We've got to get her out."

Peter told Mama's son to run to the clinic and tell Nurse Barbara that they would be bringing Dr. Alicia in.

The rain swelled to a deluge but the rescuers were able to evacuate Alicia to the clinic in less than an hour. Peter detoured them around Mango's body on the way in and on the way out.

Nurse Barbara was experienced with traumatic injuries, but the clinic had no X-ray machine. She excused Ramona, John, Peter, and Leonard and took over Alicia's care.

Mama Bernard invited the rescue party to the inn for some food and drink. Kinihira's street was jammed with excited onlookers. Rumors spread wildly. Many thought that Dr. Alicia had tangled with the poachers, maybe even with the American girl's kidnappers.

"We have to go back to check on Bee," Ramona told Peter, as they finished their coffee and cookies. "She's still my patient."

Chapter 67) Searching for Bee

Peter and Ramona dug a hole to store Mango's body until they could move him to Ruhengiri for an autopsy. There was little doubt about the cause of death: blood loss. Neither had ever seen such mutilation.

"Now Bee," Ramona said.

They trudged the trails in pouring rain for several hours, but the chimpanzees were not to be found. Peter and Ramona returned to the field station at dusk.

Leonard met them. "Nurse Barbara says that we'll be able to see Alicia by evening. I made water for showers."

It was Ramona's turn to borrow clothes. Leonard laid out some of Alicia's sweats, socks, and slippers and took Ramona's field clothes for a badly needed wash. He set her boots near the fire to dry. Peter decided to go home to clean up.

Ramona, Peter, and John met at the clinic at 6 p.m.

Alicia was in a bed, covered with clean white sheets and two gray blankets. Her face was swollen and badly bruised, but Nurse Barbara had been able to remove most of trail rash that had been embedded in her forehead and cheeks. She had lost a second tooth, both uppers, right in the front of her mouth.

"She's got a huge bruise on her left thigh, and her left knee is badly swollen. There are no breaks that I could see but she hit something or something hit her hard in that leg," said Barbara.

"She was slammed into a tree trunk," said Peter, purposely not identifying the slammer.

"Her right ankle is also badly swollen and bruised. She didn't have a boot on her right foot," said Barbara.

"She was dragged by her right foot until she hit the tree. The boot came off."

"I need to tell you that I had to call the police because this was such a violent attack."

"No need for that," said Alicia weakly. "How's Bee?" The "s" in "How's" whistled out of her mouth.

"We couldn't find any of the chimpanzees this afternoon," said Peter. "Probably sheltering from the rain. But Rain was holding her when we last saw her this morning. I'm sure I got it on video."

"She could be lying out there in the rain," said Alicia, with another whistling "s".

"We'll start before dawn tomorrow. Maybe Ja will show up."

"Mango? I heard screaming," asked Alicia.

"Dead," said Peter.

"She needs to rest now," said Nurse Barbara. "I gave her a sedative and a painkiller."

Alicia had already fallen asleep. The group went to the waiting area.

"Here's her clothes," said Nurse Barbara. "Bring her something warm and loose to wear. She'll be here at least another day, and then she should go to the hospital in

Gisenyi to get checked over by a doctor. Come back around 10 in the morning."

"Did anybody pick up her other boot?" asked Peter.

Chapter 68) Nineteen

Nineteen chimpanzees had been living in the Gishwati forest at dawn yesterday, and 19 lived there this morning, but much had changed.

Peter and Ramona searched for two hours before finding the chimpanzees. They finally spotted a tight cluster of 17 nests in the pre-dawn light. The rain had stopped and the clouds were floating off in wispy strings.

"Are you worried about another attack?" Ramona asked Peter.

"No. The only attack yesterday was by Mango, and he's dead," said Peter. "If I give you the names of the chimps as they get up, will you write them down?" Peter handed Ramona the notebook.

Stone was the first to leave the nest. Bee was not with him. Rain was the thirteenth to rise, and little Bee, dry and sleepy-eyed, was clinging tightly to her. They all peed and pooped. Peter and Ramona smiled and quietly high-fived. A tear formed in Peter's eye.

"Looks like they're headed to the bamboo to eat," said Peter. "Let's focus on Bee."

They were further relieved to see Rain strip some bamboo shoots and offer them to Bee. But the shoots were tough and hard to chew with baby teeth. Stone came to her with a huge wadge of pre-chewed bamboo. Bee tore in. Rain got the idea of pre-chewing food for Bee.

Bee sought Rain's nipple, but nursing was beyond the range of her sisterly capabilities. Bee whined. Potato ran over, somersaulted and slapped Bee on the shoulder, triggering a quick game of chase and tickle. The sun broke through the still-dripping trees, and all of the apes separated into small groups for grooming and drying out.

Potato returned to Squash for a motherly cuddle and suck. Stone scooped Bee up and began to play with her. He was soon tickling Bee behind the knees. She chuckled uncontrollably.

Stone scooped Bee up once again, this time depositing her in Squash's lap. Potato was nursing on Squash's left nipple. Bee could not resist the pendulous right nipple. Squash lifted her right arm to brush Bee off, but Stone gently grasped her wrist and stared intently into her eyes. Potato now had a stepsister. The two sometimes squabbled over nipples but Squash soon learned to ration her milk. Both would be weaned in several months, early by chimpanzee schedules.

Stone strode off purposively a few minutes later. He had a promise to keep.

Chapter 69) Guilt and Innocence

Lieutenant Habimana had already interviewed Alicia by the time Peter and Ramona arrived at the clinic at 10 a.m., still muddy and wet from their trip to the forest.

"How's Bee?" asked Alicia. Ramona filled her in on the morning's wonderful news.

"Dr. Oliveira does not remember what happened to her," said the lieutenant. "She says she was attacked by a chimpanzee."

"That's true," said Peter.

"I want to interview you each separately."

"Maybe watching a video will save you some time," said Peter.

"I want to see it too," said Alicia.

Habimana, Ramona, and Peter sat on the edge of Alicia's bed, the four of them peering at the small screen of Peter's camera.

The video showed Alicia taking Bee out of the bag, Thistle's approach, Bee's scream and frantic clinging to Alicia, Stone's approach, Alicia's being knocked down, and Stone's taking Bee up a tree.

"Hold it there," said the lieutenant. "Is that the attack?"

"I'll replay it and slow it down. Look carefully," said Peter.

The slow-motion replay showed convincingly that, while Stone's rush had knocked Alicia backward, he had not intentionally hit her.

"So who attacked her?" asked the lieutenant.

Peter restarted the video, at normal speed. It showed Rain approaching Stone and Bee up in the tree, and Bee eventually climbing on to Rain. Then there was a blur.

"When I heard Alicia yell, I turned to see what was happening on the ground. I kept the camera going," said Peter.

Peter had missed Ramona and John helping Alicia to her feet after Stone had knocked her over, the beginning of Mango's attack, and the first part of his dragging Alicia. When the scene stabilized and re-focused, Mango had already changed direction and was dragging Alicia up the trail by one foot. The jarring collision with the fallen log was shown clearly, as was Mango's stomping on her. The video then became a blurred and bumpy picture of the ground as Peter ran toward Alicia.

"So which chimpanzee is that?" asked Habimana.

"We call him Mango," said Alicia.

"Why did he attack you?"

"We'll never know."

"Was your pygmy there?"

"No, we haven't seen him for days," said Peter.

"Could he have been, like, controlling this chimpanzee, somehow getting him, training him, to attack you?" asked the lieutenant.

"Not a chance," said Alicia firmly.

"This ape is dangerous. He could attack others. We have to kill it. It's like the dogs."

"What dogs?" asked Alicia.

"During the genocide, society broke down. Dogs were abandoned, and the only thing they had to eat were dead bodies, dead human bodies, and there were so many bodies that they couldn't all be buried," said the lieutenant. "The dogs developed a taste for human flesh," he continued. "By the time peace came, the dogs had become savage, roaming in packs. They had to be killed. Every last dog was shot or poisoned. That was almost 20 years ago and we still don't have many dogs in Rwanda, and we don't like them."

"But the dogs were doing what they needed to do to survive," said Alicia. "Mango did not have to attack me to survive."

"Exactly. That's why we have to kill him," said Habimana

"You mean to punish him?" said Alicia, in an argumentative tone.

"Let me remind you, Dr. Oliveira, that you're the one who says that chimpanzees can be murdered and kidnapped, and that the *people* who are responsible should be punished, kept from doing it again. You can't have it both ways. In your terms, this would be a felonious assault on a person by a chimpanzee, maybe two chimpanzees. They have to be kept from assaulting others. Prison is not an option. They have to be killed."

Ramona and Peter were speechless.

"Let me remind you, Lieutenant, that you're the one who said that chimpanzees are animals, and they can only be killed or stolen, not murdered or kidnapped like people. If they're not like people, then they can't commit crimes like people, they should not be judged like people, and they should not be punished like people."

She pressed on: "Actually, you said the chimpanzees were Rwanda's property. Maybe it's their owners who should be punished."

"Stop!" said Ramona, in a loud and forceful voice. "You're giving me a headache. We don't have to resolve this philosophically. The apes killed Mango."

"You mean... "

"I only mean that they killed him. Savagely, as if he were a stranger," said Ramona. "I'll have an autopsy report for you in a week."

"What about the other one, the leader?" asked the lieutenant.

"He did not attack me. He just came to rescue his baby and knocked me down accidentally," said Alicia.

"I need some time to think about all of this," said the lieutenant. "I'll ask Kanoro what he thinks, since he's responsible for this forest."

"Aren't you happy that Bee is back with her family?" asked Alicia. "You're responsible for that you know."

"Thanks, I'll tell Kanoro about that too."

"Give him my regards," said Alicia.

Chapter 70) Another Message from Stone

Alicia was released from the clinic at noon, with orders to rest and walk only with crutches. She was to see a doctor in Gisenyi as soon as the swelling in her knee and ankle had gone down. Under no circumstance was she to go into the forest.

Ramona drove Alicia to the field station and left her in Leonard's care.

"I need to get back to the clinic in Ruhengiri," Ramona told Alicia. "Is it OK if Peter helps John and I dig up Mango's body and get it into our van?"

"Of course. Thank you for everything, girl," said Alicia.

"Here. I owe you a whole bag of chocolates."

Ramona parked the Gorilla Doctors van at the trailhead. Peter recruited a few helpers, and they dug up Mango's body and placed it on the stretcher. Peter gingerly placed the dismembered male parts on his chest. The helpers exchanged troubled looks, and then started to carry the stretcher to the road, Peter touched Ramona on the shoulder and signaled her to lag behind.

"Look," he whispered.

Alicia's right boot hung from a broken branch at shoulder height. The broken-off end of the branch laid on the ground below.

"My God," said Ramona. "Who could have left this here? Your missing Batwa assistant?"

"Ja's strong but not strong enough to break off that branch. He would have cut it off with his machete."

"Who then?"

"Stone."

"The chimp returned the shoe?"

"He's apologizing."

"No way," said Ramona. "I know gorillas, and they would never, could never, do that."

"Do your gorillas know right from wrong?" asked Peter.

"No... well, yes... for some things, but they'd never apologize."

"Amazing what a few different strands of DNA can do," said Peter, slipping the shoe off the branch.

By the time Peter and Ramona returned to the road, John had supervised the loading of Mango's body into the van. It was beginning to smell. He covered it with a tarp. Peter hugged Ramona, braced shoulders with John, and watched as they drove off.

Only then did he fish the piece of soggy, dirty paper out of the boot. Bee's and Stone's faces, united in a scarlet circle, stared back at him. They looked to be almost smiling.

She'd never *believe this*, Peter thought.

Chapter 71) Escape

Elizabeth had been held in the cave for a week, and had been alone for the last 24 hours. Her clothes hung on her like Ja's Bar Mitzvah shirt. She had gathered her filthy hair into a knotted ponytail to keep it out of her face. What had been attractively prominent cheekbones now jutted unpleasantly over her pale, hunger-sunken face. Broken, dirty fingernails; chapped lips; fuzzy teeth and tongue; blood- and sweat-stained clothes; and itchy feet that signaled a fungus spreading in her damp boots rounded out the picture of a desperate crone.

She could no longer stay clean with the cave's trickles of cold water, and she was losing her motivation even to try. She was desperately hungry. She missed the kindness and company of the chimpanzees, who had now abandoned her.

"OK, it's time. I've got to get out of here," she resolved, out loud.

The sun was high as she inched her way out of the cave entrance. Ja missed her emergence because he was dozing at his lookout point in the forest after the wet night. The chimpanzees were on the other side of the ridge, quietly indulging in Bee's return.

She considered her options as her eyes adjusted to the light: *Must be 30 feet straight down. Can't even see the bottom. Not possible. There's nothing to hold on to. Can't cross the waterfall. They walked me in on that little crack going the other way, but I'll never get past that big stone without help. What's up there?*

She looked up. A rounded boulder overhung the cave entrance but she could glimpse a small grassy clearing above. She scanned for overhanging branches but they were too distant for her to reach.

I've got to get up and over that stone, now, before I lose any more strength.

She extended her arm and probed for a handhold at the top of the sun-warmed boulder. She tried lifting her weight on one arm and hand. The friction of her body sliding on the stone kept her from moving upward. She tried adding the other arm, and found a grip. Standing on tiptoes, she began to pull herself up. Her chest inched slowly upward. Her feet now dangled uselessly. She flung her right leg up and around, searching for a needed foothold. Her fingers began to ache.

"No!" she said fiercely, but her will was no match for the physics of her predicament. A picture flashed through her mind of dropping, missing the ledge in front of the cave, and crashing to the cobbled riverbank, 30 feet below.

A massive, calloused hand closed around her wrist and began to pull her up, slowly, almost gently, but with unfailing strength. Elizabeth went along for the ride. She saw brow ridges first, then the big ears and deep brown eyes, and finally the graying visage of the male who had engineered her kidnapping in the first place. She had not seen much of him since but knew that he had the bearing of a leader. Stone pulled Elizabeth to her feet at the top of Kazaneza Falls.

"Thank you." *Now what?* she thought.

Stone's stare was warm and friendly. He cocked his head in friendly fashion and squeaked happily.

Thank God it's not the nasty one.

Chapter 72) Peter's Dilemma Continues

Peter handed the boot to Alicia, who was sitting in the late afternoon sun in the yard of the field station.

"I found it in the forest." This was true, but it was also a lie by omission. He didn't tell her that it had been left on a broken limb for him to find.

There were other such lies. Peter had still not told Alicia that he knew who had kidnapped Elizabeth and why, and that he had a pretty good idea of where she was being held. He also had not told her that he had been "communicating" with Stone. He was not about to tell her any of this yet. He wanted to give Stone's plan a little more time to unfold, but wondered if Stone would, or could, actually keep his end of the trade. Could Stone truly understand that he should return Elizabeth now that Bee had been returned? If not, Peter would have to intervene, and soon.

"So you think chimpanzees know right from wrong?" said Peter, as more of a hopeful conclusion than a question.

"Of course. They do some things that we consider to be wrong, but they're right in their own terms. They steal some food from farmers because they're hungry, but it's the farmers who cut down the forest and caused a shortage of natural foods," said Alicia.

"What about Mango's baby-shaking? Why did he do that?"

"That was wrong. Mango seemed to cross the line frequently."

"Was it wrong that he attacked you?"

"Maybe he misunderstood, and thought that I had kidnapped Bee."

"But you had already given her back. She was with the group."

"I know. I don't really understand why he did what he did," said Alicia.

"Was it wrong for the chimps to kill Mango?"

"I don't know. I guess it depends on why he attacked me or what else he might have done. What's with all of the questions, anyway?"

"Your conversation with Habimana at the clinic this morning set my head spinning. You said that chimpanzees could not commit a crime, and that they should not be judged or punished by people for what they do. But just now, you said they know the difference between right and wrong."

"So... ?"

"To me, if they do something intentionally that they know is wrong, then they can be judged and maybe punished," said Peter.

"You know, we wouldn't be having this conversation if we were studying servals. The apes are so humanlike, so smart, so emotionally like us that we seem to regard them as humans sometimes and as animals at other times."

"Where's the line?"

"I don't know but I do know that it would be wrong for

Habimana or Kanoro to punish these chimpanzees, or exterminate them like dogs," said Alicia.

"For anything?"

"Like what?" asked Alicia.

Peter wanted to say: "Suppose they kidnapped a person?" but he decided not to go there yet.

"So it was OK to punish the Chen woman for having Apple killed and taking Bee, but it wouldn't be OK to punish Mango for attacking you?" asked Peter.

"The chimpanzees punished him. Anyway, Peter, I guess I'm not consistent about this," said Alicia. "I just want to protect those chimpanzees. And I want to get on with my work."

"I'm with you there," said Peter.

"I've got nine more days to shut this place down and go back to Brazil," said Alicia. "Now I at least have an excuse to leave... I need to go home for medical treatment. Maybe I can salvage my career yet. I'll ask the Ark foundation to continue to support your and Ja's salary. Not sure what I can do for Leonard."

"It would probably help if Elizabeth were found," said Peter.

"That's for sure, but it looks more hopeless every day," said Alicia.

"Miracles happen," said Peter. He had much better reason than Alicia to hope for a "miracle," but her safe return was still a long shot. And Peter would be at fault if Elizabeth were not found quickly.

He was tempted to go back into the forest to see what was happening, but it would be getting dark soon.

Chapter 73) Procession

Stone solemnly extended his hand to Elizabeth, palm down. She touched the back of his hand, still grateful that he had rescued her.

He grasped her wrist and began to walk on three limbs, leading Elizabeth gently by the hand, away from her jail.

He smells better than I do, thought Elizabeth.

Stone seemed to recognize that Elizabeth was weakened by hunger and fatigue, and stiff from lack of exercise. He moved slowly, picking the route that was the easiest for the girl. They went to the top of the falls and crossed the river. Elizabeth stumbled on a slippery rock. Stone was there to catch her.

Quite different from the last time this guy and I crossed the river.

Rain and Thistle were waiting on the other side. Squash appeared.

"Where'd you get another baby?" Elizabeth asked. She

couldn't help but smile at the four pink, protruding ears. Rain took over carrying Bee to help Squash out on the rest of the trip.

Elizabeth's thoughts were swirling: *Where are they taking me? Why are they moving me? What would happen if I walked in another direction? Why am I trusting them?*

All nineteen of the Gishwati chimpanzees had soon joined the procession. They were in front of Elizabeth, behind her, over her, beside her, but they weren't herding her. She felt a little like a queen with an escort, though she decidedly did not look or smell like a queen.

Ja materialized. "Hello, Lizbeth. You OK?"

"I'm OK. How are you?" she asked, looking at his still-splinted wrist.

"Hurts when I walk but I'm OK."

"Do you know where we're going?"

"Home, I think."

"Are you coming with us? You have to get your wrist in a real cast."

"No, not out of the forest."

"Why not?"

"Police are looking for me. Now they will think that I took you."

"But I'll tell them ..."

"They won't believe you."

Elizabeth realized that probably nobody, not even her mother, would ever believe the true story of her kidnapping.

But who, she wondered, had sent the food in the newspaper? That was not the work of the apes. Dr. Oliveira? Had she helped the apes? Put them up to it? Could she even do that? And why would she?

The group detoured around the place where Mango had died. It had become a taboo location, although Stone had hung Alicia's boot there yesterday for Peter to find.

Night was falling as the procession started up the final hill. The apes and Ja risked going to within 50 feet of the road. Elizabeth labored just to put one foot in front of the other as she walked the steep final stretch, but she was energized at the prospect of freedom.

"Go there," said Ja, pointing up the trail. "Close now. Turn this way on road," he said, pointing left.

Chapter 74) Elizabeth Reintroduced

Mama Bernard's son was walking home from school in the late afternoon as the haggard American emerged from the forest. He got over the shock quickly.

"Do you speak English?" he asked.

He took Elizabeth directly to his mother at the inn. Mama, uncharacteristically, lost her composure and was momentarily speechless.

She recovered in seconds: "Holy God, thank you."

Mama took Elizabeth by the hand and led her across the street to the field station. Peter was just coming out of the gate on his way home.

The surge of adrenalin was so strong that he could feel the pupils of his eyes dilate.

"Good God, it's you."

Peter was awash in joy that Stone (and maybe Ja, if he were also responsible) had kept the promise. The girl was back, he might be freed of guilt, and he might even have a job.

"*Meu Deus*," said Alicia, when Peter led Elizabeth to her. "Are you OK? You look awful."

"You don't look so good yourself, Dr. Oliveira."

Alicia stood unsteadily on her crutches and embraced Elizabeth. The girl was greasy and smelled bad, but Alicia was delighted to see her.

Mama Bernard, still in the street, was calling her sister in Gisenyi to send food and drink up the mountain as soon as possible. She sensed that Kinihira would soon be transformed, yet again.

"I need to call my mom," said Elizabeth, taking out her phone. "Crap, no battery."

"Use mine. I have to call the police afterward."

"Oh my God!" screamed Kim Weatherby, in a voice that could be heard by anybody in Kinihira who was within 25 feet of the phone. "Are you OK? Where were you?"

Elizabeth broke into tears. "I'm OK, mommy, but I want to come home."

"Where are you?"

"At the field station."

"Go to the police now. You can't trust those people. I still think they might have been involved in your disappearance."

"We're going to call the police now," said Elizabeth.

"There's a lieutenant. Martin somebody. Ask for him. Don't leave the field station until he gets there."

"Mommy, bring me fresh clothes and a toothbrush and shampoo and pizza. Lots of pizza."

"I've been waiting for this moment for a week. Your bag is all packed. I'll leave as soon as I can get a car."

Elizabeth ended the call and handed the phone back to Alicia.

"I need a Coke," said Elizabeth, "and then a shower."

"I'm already heating the water," said Leonard.

"Mama Bernard doesn't have Coke but she has Fanta. I'll be right back," said Peter.

Chapter 75) Stuck in Kigali

"Lieutenant, this is Alicia Oliveira."

"What now?"

"Elizabeth is back. We're at the field station."

"Is she OK?"

"I think so."

"Damn. I'm in Kigali for training but I'll come right back. I'll be there by 10 tonight. Close that gate and keep it closed."

"She's already called her mother. I'll leave a message for Kanoro."

"Let me do that," said the lieutenant.

Unknown to any of them, a tank truck carrying a load of diesel fuel to the Goma airport had at that moment lost its brakes on a downhill section of the only road between Kigali and Gisenyi. It gathered ferocious speed, jackknifed, and slid sideways for 300 feet, wiping out dozens of homebound pedestrians on both sides of the road like bowling pins. The truck finally flipped and burst into flames. Many were killed and injured, some crushed, others burned alive. The road would be closed for the next 14 hours.

Kim Weatherby, Martin Habimana, and Olivier Kanoro would spend the night in Kigali. No helicopter would be recalled from Sudan to take them to Kinihira.

Chapter 76) Cleaning Up

"Don't even bother washing these," Elizabeth told Leonard, as she handed him her clothes from behind the cracked-open door of the shower stall. Steam was rising from the pails of hot water that Leonard had set inside.

"Oh, we've seen worse," said Leonard, passing her a folded pile of one of Alicia's fluffy white towels, a sweatshirt and sweat pants, and a pair of flip-flops.

Elizabeth lathered, scrubbed, and rinsed for four cycles and toweled herself off. She donned the sweats, which hung on her emaciated frame, and emerged from the stall, fragrant and flushed.

She scrubbed her teeth furiously at the outdoor faucet with a borrowed toothbrush, and then walked to the dining room, idly combing her squeaky blond hair with her fingers.

"Let's eat," said Alicia. While Leonard was serving, Elizabeth used the tattered fingernails of her right hand to dig the last of the grime from beneath the nails of her left, and then reversed hands. Peter and Alicia found this bit of hygiene unappetizing. Peter knew that Elizabeth had not had human dining companions for some time.

There was much to be said at supper but Elizabeth did not waste a breath on talking. She shoveled down brown beans, boiled potatoes, and macaroni and tomato sauce, the typical carb-rich, meatless diet of rural Rwandans. There was also, at Alicia's insistence, a fresh mixed salad. Mama sent her son over with a zucchini cake and three more Fantas.

"We're charging your phone," said Peter.

"The lieutenant called me while you were in the shower," said Alicia. "There's been an accident on the highway. The road is closed. Nobody will get over here from Kigali tonight."

Elizabeth tore into the cake. Peter and Alicia picked at their food, bursting with unasked questions.

It was Elizabeth who broke the silence: "What happened to you?" she asked Alicia.

"I was attacked by a chimpanzee."

"I was too," said Elizabeth. "But I got off easier than you.

That little guy, Ja, saved me."

"So it was Ja that kidnapped you?" asked Alicia.

"No!" Elizabeth's response was emphatic.

"Is Ja OK?" asked Peter.

"He has a broken wrist but I sort of set it," said Elizabeth.

"So what happened to you?" asked Alicia.

"Can I go to sleep now?"

"It's only 6:30. Do you want to go to the clinic?"

"Really, I'm just exhausted. Can we talk in the morning?"

Peter was grateful that he would have the night in his own bed to figure out what he was going to say to whom the next morning.

Chapter 77) Confession

Peter showed up early for breakfast.

"We need to talk, before the people from Kigali get here," he said to Alicia.

"Don't tell me you're involved," said Alicia.

"In a way, yes." Peter went on to tell Alicia that he had

known for five days that it had been the chimpanzees that had kidnapped Alicia, and that he had known that they had taken her to trade for Bee. He told her that Ja knew about it also, and that Ja and he were providing some food for Elizabeth. He told her also about his clumsy attempts to communicate with Stone.

"Peter, you knew about a crime and didn't tell me or the police?"

"Let's talk later about whether this was a crime or not, but yes, I knew about it and didn't tell anybody."

"Why not? She could have died."

"I know, I know. Ja was telling me that Elizabeth was OK. I was going to call Lieutenant Habimana, but then we found Bee and I thought the plan, Stone's plan, might just work."

"Did Ja help with the kidnapping?" asked Alicia.

"He says he didn't, and I believe him. We both helped, though, by getting food to her and not speaking up."

"Did you know where they were keeping her?"

Peter initially fell back on plausible denial: "No. Ja knew, but he didn't tell me."

Then he decided to get it all out: "I had a pretty good idea though. There's a cave that we have not shown you. It's right next to Kazaneza Falls. You've walked right past it dozens of times. The chimpanzees and Batwa use it to get salt and minerals to eat. I should have told you this, but it's sort of sacred, a secret of The Past Times. I discovered it when I was a boy, watching the chimpanzees."

"That's an important piece for my study."

"I've felt really guilty about not telling you."

"I understand. This *is* your home, your history. I'm just passing through."

"I have been disloyal to you. I don't know what more to say."

"Let's move on, Peter. You've been an ideal assistant in every other way. What made you think that the chimpanzees could come up with a ransom plan?"

"Actually, you did. Remember our talks about the chimpanzees' trading meat for sex? Trading bananas for rakes? Popsicles for light bulbs, when they wouldn't settle for a banana? In Stone's mind, this was a trade. Elizabeth for Bee."

"But the people who had Bee did not want Elizabeth, and Mrs. Weatherby didn't have Bee."

"I'm guessing now, but in Stone's small world, Bee had to be nearby and the people who wanted Elizabeth back had to know where Bee was," said Peter.

"But it worked," said Alicia. "Stone's assumption was wrong, but we did find Bee.

"And if we had not been able to return Bee to the group, I would have had to tell the police, and you, that I knew about Elizabeth," said Peter.

"So what do we tell the police now?" asked Alicia. "You and Ja knew about the kidnapping."

"We didn't kidnap her," said Peter. "We helped Elizabeth, not the chimpanzees."

"I hope Habimana and Kanoro will see it like that," said Alicia.

"Do we have to tell them?"

"Hmm. It is Elizabeth's story to tell," said Alicia.

Chapter 78) Elizabeth's Story

Elizabeth came into the dining room, refreshed by a night's sleep in a soft bed. She asked if she could take another shower. Leonard had the water ready. He had also washed and dried her clothes and boots. There were still a few ground-in stains but the clothes were otherwise clean and smelling of soap and mountain air.

Alicia pressed some coffee. Leonard made oatmeal and *igikoma*, and set out jam and honey and the leftover zucchini cake. Elizabeth, fresh from the shower, ate with overflowing spoonfuls, the white towel wrapped turban-like around her head.

"I almost feel human again," she said.

"As opposed to feeling... how?" asked Alicia. "Peter has been telling me what he knows about what happened to you. That the chimpanzees kidnapped you."

"I can barely believe it myself," said Elizabeth. "But they were nice to me, all except one."

"How, exactly did they kidnap you? Did they pick you up and carry you?"

"No, there were four of them and they just surrounded me and forced me to walk in one direction. They didn't touch me, just kind of herded me, to a cave. One, the leader male I think, led me by the hand across the rocks to the cave."

"You realize that nobody will believe you," said Alicia. "I trust Peter, I know how smart chimpanzees are, and *I* barely believe the story."

Peter detected a new tone in Alicia's voice, a tone of resolve, of taking charge.

"My mother will believe me."

"Maybe, but maybe she'll think you took off for a fling with a Rwandan. You look pretty good right now. Not like you've been through an ordeal."

"Are you suggesting that I should lie about what happened?"

"Not at all," said Alicia. "It's your story to tell."

"So what then?" asked Elizabeth.

"Maybe you'd want to wait a while to tell it."

"How could I do that?"

"You have been missing for a week. You're exhausted, you're not feeling well, you can't remember much right now."

"Lieutenant Habimana will ask her about Ja, about whether Ja was involved," said Peter.

"He wasn't!" snapped Elizabeth. "He saved me from that awful ape."

"What ape?" asked Peter and Alicia, in unison.

"Not the boss ape, but another big male. Kind of creepy, slimy. He licked my face and then tried to take my pants off."

"Mango," said Peter.

"Ja jumped him and pulled him off. The ape threw him, broke his wrist, cut his head. Then the chimp ran away."

"That's why Mango was missing and alone," said Peter. "Stone would have to punish him for touching Elizabeth and hurting Ja."

"If we're thinking of the same male, he's the one that attacked me too," said Alicia.

"He must have gone crazy," said Peter. Neither he nor Alicia realized at that point that Mango had been trying to ingratiate himself with Stone by attacking Alicia. They did realize that Mango's attack on Elizabeth was perverse.

"He was the only one who wasn't nice to me. Where's my phone? I've got some pictures of some of the others. There was an adorable baby. Actually, when they brought me out of the woods, I saw two babies, but I only have a picture of one. "

"That second baby is why you were kidnapped, and why you were returned," said Alicia. She proceeded to tell Elizabeth the ransom story and about Bee's return, Mango's attack on her, and his subsequent "execution." Alicia emphasized the quotation marks by raising her hands and wiggling her index and middle fingers in the air.

"And you're telling me that nobody will believe *my* story? You've got a whopper there too," said Elizabeth.

"If I told your story, I'd never be taken seriously as a scientist again," said Alicia. "Animal rights people would love it, but I'd be a nutcase to my colleagues. I think we both have good reasons to say as little as we can at this point."

More lies by omission, thought Peter.

Chapter 79) Reunion

Cat strode from the forest into the bamboo grove on his stilt-like legs. The chimpanzees looked up from their bamboo shoots, perplexed by the confidence of the cat's approach. Chicken and Fig had never eaten serval but they quickly began to scheme. Stone stopped playing with Bee and drew her to him protectively, but she squirmed away and ran toward Cat. Stone was stunned, and he hesitated for one heartbeat. Cat jumped straight up and landed on the incoming Bee, who started to chuckle: "*heh...heh...heh...heh.*" Bee grabbed Cat on his way back to earth and pulled him to his side. The two began to wrestle. Stone sensed that all of this was OK, and the rest of the group relaxed as well.

Ja, who had been observing the chimpanzees while waiting for Peter, found himself smiling. He had seen chimpanzees play, but never with a different kind of animal. He asked himself how these two could know each other. Stone was thinking the same thing.

Even more amazing to Ja was that Bee was with the group. He had been so occupied with looking after Elizabeth, and his movement had been so restricted due to his injury, that he had little idea of the events of the past two days. He was so absorbed that he did not even hear Peter's approach.

"How is your arm?"

"Good. Less pain. Still weak."

"You should not be using it."

"I need two hands to climb trees."

"Stay on the ground for a while."

"Bee is back. Do you know how?" asked Ja.

Peter filled him in on Bee's recovery and release.

"Can you see Bee and this serval play?" asked Ja.

"Look for a tattoo on the serval's leg. Bee was with a serval when we found her in Goma. We released the serval in the forest the same day we released Bee."

"How is Lizbeth?"

"OK, cleaned up and fed. She is very thankful for your help."

"Mango attacked her. Not bite. Love attack. Wrong. I stopped him."

"Mango also attacked Alicia," Peter said. He described the actual moments of Bee's release and the subsequent events.

"They kill Mango?" Ja asked, for confirmation.

"The chimps did. Very violently."

"How is Dr. Alicia?"

"She's OK, but she can't come into the forest. The minister is making her go home next week. We may not have jobs."

"Do the police know the chimpanzees kidnapped Lizbeth?" asked Ja.

"No, not yet, but the lieutenant is coming soon."

"Ja will stay hiding in the forest," said Ja.

"Elizabeth has told us what you did to help and protect her, and I'm sure she will tell the police."

"But you and me both knew where she was," said Ja.

"Yes, that's a problem," said Peter. "I guess we sort of helped the chimpanzees as well as Elizabeth."

Potato tried to join the play bout but both Cat and Bee ignored him. Potato ran crying to Squash. Stone stood up, recognizing the unfairness. The game was over, the mood broken.

Cat took a long look at Bee and slipped back into the forest.

Chapter 80) Another Reunion

Augustin was accustomed to taking tourists to their wildlife treks at the crack of dawn. He picked up Kim Weatherby at her Kigali apartment at 5:30 a.m. and headed to Gishwati. Olivier Kanoro was not even out of bed yet. Martin Habimana had taken a bus to Kigali for his training a few days earlier, and he was now trying to borrow a car from the Kigali city police to get back to Kinihira.

It was a slow trip for Augustin and Weatherby. The burned and twisted chassis of the tank truck had been moved to the side of the road, and thousands of onlookers and mourners had gathered at the accident scene. The police had managed to open two lanes, but the crush of people spilled over onto the highway.

Augustin and Kim Weatherby made it to Kinihira at 10:30. Elizabeth bounded out of the field station as the Land Cruiser came through the gate.

"Mommy, mommy," cried Elizabeth, as she buried her face in her mother's neck. Prior to last night, she had not called her mother "mommy" for fifteen years. But, at this moment, her need for comfort and safety was primordial, and Kim Weatherby noticed.

They embraced for such a long time that Alicia was able to hobble out of the dining room into the yard, wincing with pain. Kim eyed her suspiciously. Elizabeth felt her mother tense.

"Mom, Dr. Oliveira had nothing to do with my disappearance. You have to believe that. These people have been fantastic."

"Then who did kidnap you?"

"Can my mom and I talk alone in the dining room?" Elizabeth asked Alicia.

"Sure. Would you like some coffee or something to eat Mrs. Weatherby?" asked Alicia.

"That would be great."

"Mom, can I call Whitney first?"

"It's the middle of the night there, but sure. Use my phone."

A few minutes later, a sleepy Whitney tweeted: "Elizabeth Weatherby found safely after a week in the Gishwati Forest. Kidnappers not yet identified." She also sent an e-mail to her contact at the *Wall Street Journal*. A short article would appear in the morning edition. President Clinton would read it with satisfaction and relief.

Chapter 81) The Truth

"That's the biggest pile of bull crap that I've ever heard, at least from you," said Kim Weatherby, after listening to her daughter for ten minutes. "That's just pure crap." She was up and pacing back and forth across the cramped dining room. "What are you trying to hide? Who are you protecting?"

"It's the truth, to the best that I can remember."

"Then your memory is not clear, not working. It's preposterous. Nobody will ever believe it. That place was crawling with cops and Rwanda's best soldiers for two days. No way you wouldn't have been found if you were in there."

"Ask Dr. Alicia. Ask Peter."

"They're part of this, Elizabeth. Their word can't be trusted."

"So, am I supposed to lie?"

"No. You'll say nothing. Nothing except that you can't remember."

"That's a lie," said Elizabeth.

"It may seem like that to you, but you'd tell me the truth if you could remember, unless... "

"Unless what?" Elizabeth said loudly.

"Did you run off with a man?"

"Mother!" said Elizabeth, stiffening and standing. Kim had gone from "Mommy" to "Mom" to "Mother" in 15 minutes.

"I'm getting you out of here. Get your stuff. There's pizza and Coke in the car."

Elizabeth did not want to leave without greater closure. But the thought of her mother's luxurious, air-conditioned apartment and the pool in Kigali was attractive.

"I guess I owe you some thanks," said Kim Weatherby to Alicia in the yard. "I'm taking Elizabeth home now."

"But Lieutenant Habimana will want to talk with her."

"She has been under great stress. She's lost her memory of the past week. She's delusional."

"I know her story is hard to believe. I barely believe it myself. Peter and my other field assistant confirm it. Given what I know about chimpanzees, it could have happened the way she remembers."

"You are all covering something up," said Mrs. Weatherby. "You're protecting somebody, or maybe even Elizabeth herself."

Augustin opened the rear doors of the Land Cruiser. Elizabeth hugged Alicia, and then she hugged Peter, who was just returning from the forest.

"If it was you that sent the food in the newspapers, thank you," she whispered in his ear.

She thanked Leonard, and got in.

Augustin started the car, but a police pickup truck, with Lieutenant Habimana in the passenger seat and eight uniformed Kigali police officers riding on bench seats in the back, pulled in front of the open gate.

Chapter 82) An Alternative Truth

Habimana stuck his head into the open rear window of the Land Cruiser.

"Good morning, Mrs. Weatherby. Elizabeth. Are you OK?"

"We are OK," said Mrs. Weatherby, "but Elizabeth is not well. She's delusional and suffering from memory loss."

"Well, I need to talk to her."

"I'm afraid that's impossible," said the woman. "I need to get her back to Kigali for a... you know... a thorough medical examination."

"Mother!" exploded Elizabeth, realizing that the intent of a "thorough" medical examination was to investigate the "ran-off-with-a-man" theory.

Alicia whispered to Peter: "I told her to wait to tell the story."

Elizabeth got out of the car, her face reddened with embarrassment and anger.

"What do you want to know, Lieutenant?" she asked.

"Let's go inside," he said.

"I'm going with her," said Mrs. Weatherby.

Habimana relented, knowing that Minister Kanoro was only 30 minutes behind him and that there were two reporters in the minister's car. He wanted to clear this up before they arrived.

"So, you look pretty good. Are you hurt or harmed in any way."

"I'm tired but OK," Elizabeth replied.

"Where have you been?"

"I don't remember."

"Did you hit your head, or were you beaten?"

"No."

"Who were you with? Were you kidnapped?"

"I don't remember."

Kim Weatherby relaxed in her chair, confident that Elizabeth had heeded her motherly advice and would not be telling her outrageous story to the police.

Habimana asked the same questions in different ways for ten more minutes, and got the same answers. He had had enough training and experience with interrogation to know that Elizabeth was sandbagging him.

"Did you see the little pygmy known as Ja?"

Elizabeth hesitated for one second too long.

"So he's your kidnapper," said Habimana with certainty. "Why are you protecting him?"

Elizabeth's eyes narrowed and she stared directly at Habimana. She sat stiffly upright in her chair, and her words became as clipped and forceful as flying bullets.

"Lieutenant Habimana, I want you to write down, *verbatim*, what I am going to tell you. You can get another policeman as a witness."

"That won't be necessary," he said.

"First, Ja did not take me. Second, he saved me, and third, he brought me back from the forest. He is a hero."

"Tell me more," said Habimana, writing quickly.

"That's all I remember right now, but I remember that, for certain. Let me sign your notebook."

"That won't be necessary either, but unless you give me more details, he will still be a person of interest."

"Dr. Alicia and Peter also did not take me. You are dead wrong if you blame Ja, Dr. Alicia, or Peter."

Habimana knew better than to ask: "Who then?"

"Let's go, Mom."

The police pickup had swung around to the front of Mama Bernard's inn, leaving the gate unblocked. The officers were eating a late breakfast. Curious villagers milled in the street.

Augustin started the car again and began to back into the street. This time it was Kanoro's 4Runner that pulled up behind him, again blocking his exit. Habimana greeted Kanoro. The reporters snapped pictures of the two of them shaking hands. Peter stood in the entrance and blocked the reporters' access to the Eco-Treks car.

Alicia quickly retreated to the field station. She did not want to be photographed on crutches or with missing teeth.

"I want to speak to the girl and her mother," demanded Kanoro.

"Good luck. She says she doesn't remember much," said Habimana.

Kanoro went to the Land Cruiser and exchanged pleasantries and expressions of concern with Mrs. Weatherby and Elizabeth.

"Can we talk?" he asked.

"There's not-" started Elizabeth. Kim squeezed her daughter's thigh, as a signal to shut up and let her handle this.

"Elizabeth needs to see a doctor in Kigali, Mr. Minister, but we can take a few minutes." Politics and the electricity contract came into play. The women got out of the car.

Kanoro skillfully wormed his way between Elizabeth and her mother and, arms around their waists, turned them toward the reporters' waiting cameras. He smiled broadly, and the women, who had been through their share of photo ops, reflexively smiled as well. Kanoro might as well have stood with his foot on Elizabeth's back; he had his trophy. The picture would be circulated by Rwandan embassies worldwide by evening. A highly placed official of the Rwandan government had solved the internationally publicized kidnapping of an American college girl and had returned her safely to her wealthy and influential mother. H.E. would be pleased.

"I look forward to seeing you again in Kigali," he said, dabbing at his perspiring brow with a crisp white handkerchief.

Augustin was finally allowed to back out and drive away.

Kanoro convened a press conference with the two reporters at Mama Bernard's inn, with as many villagers' ears in attendance as the little bar could hold. He said that Elizabeth had almost certainly been kidnapped by a Chinese national who had subsequently been deported for wildlife smuggling. The smuggler's former assistants, seeking to avoid capture as the Rwandan police were closing in after excellent investigative work, had snuck Elizabeth back into the Gishwati Forest and released her.

The story was plausible. It and the trophy photo were added to the *Wall Street Journal's* story, and appeared in countless other dailies in Rwanda and worldwide. Gishwati was on the map. Kanoro was a star.

Chapter 83) The Whole Truth, Almost

"What on earth happened to *you*?" Kanoro asked Alicia.

"If you really want to know, the two of you should come in and sit down," said Alicia. "The lieutenant has already heard some of what I'm going to tell you."

The three of them retired to the dining room. Alicia pressed coffee. Leonard put out some of Mama Bernard's butter cookies.

Alicia went over Bee's recovery and reintroduction, and the attack by Mango.

"That's touching," said Kanoro. "What does it have to do with Elizabeth?"

"The chimpanzees kidnapped Elizabeth and held her in a secret cave as ransom for Bee. They released her when Bee was returned. I know, Mr. Minister, that this is hard to believe, but I think that's the way it happened. So does Peter."

"Did you know about this?" Habimana asked Alicia.

"No, absolutely not," said Alicia, "not before this morning." Alicia chose not to mention that Peter and Ja had known. Fortunately, neither the minister nor the lieutenant asked about Peter or Ja.

The minister's phone rang. He got up, took a few steps away, and answered.

After a moment, he said: "Yes sir, it's true. She's OK and on her way back to Kigali with her mother." There was another pause, while he listened.

"No arrests, but we think it was the Chinese woman." Pause.

"No, we don't think the Brazilian or her staff were directly involved. Maybe one of her Batwa assistants helped in some way." Pause.

"The Brazilian was attacked by a chimpanzee but she will recover. I'll give her a few more days to pack up. No other injuries, except to one chimpanzee." Pause.

"Thank you sir." He was smiling broadly now. "The police and the RDF helped. They should get a lot of the credit." Pause.

"Thank you again sir. Good bye."

Kanoro hung up and said to Alicia and Habimana: "H.E." As if they hadn't known.

"As you heard Dr. Oliveira, I'm sticking to the far more plausible explanation for the kidnapping, the one that implicates Madam Chen. It doesn't matter anyway, since you'll be gone in a week or so and this will all die down."

Alicia fixed Kanoro's eyes.

"Mr. Minister, it's not in my interest to tell the true story at this point. But if you force me to discontinue my work here, or if you threaten these chimpanzees, I will tell the world that this group of chimpanzees made monkeys out of two crack RDF brigades and a combat helicopter flown by your first female pilots. Some people won't believe me, but the story alone will make you, H.E., and Rwanda the laughing stock of the tabloid world."

"The Weatherby girl will tell it anyway," Kanoro spluttered.

"Not for a while. Maybe in a few months, and nobody will care by then. Besides, she's a college kid. I'm a published primatologist. The world will believe me. I'm a phone call away from the *Wall Street Journal* and a keystroke from Facebook."

She and Kanoro locked eyes for several seconds. Habimana held his breath.

"Lieutenant, please come to my car with me," snapped Kanoro.

Alicia exhaled loudly after they left.

Leonard and Peter peeked around from the outdoor kitchen, where they had been eavesdropping: "Wow!"

"I can't believe I did that. They're probably going to throw me in jail."

Chapter 84) Nothing But The Truth

"I can't believe you did that," Habimana said to Alicia. "You backed down a Rwandan cabinet minister."

"What did he say out there?"

"Three things. Neither of us ever repeats a word of that conversation, you can continue your work, and it would not be in Rwanda's interest as an environmentally responsible nation to harm these apes."

Peter and Leonard, once again pressed against the wall around the corner, could barely contain themselves.

"Kanoro came out of this as a big winner. H.E. and the world think he solved the kidnapping. Everybody came out alive. He does not want you or anybody else to spoil his victory. That's why he backed down. But you and I aren't done, Dr. Oliveira," said Habimana.

For a moment, Alicia thought Martin Habimana was going to ask her out.

"My job is to solve crimes and catch criminals, not return lost girls to their mothers."

"What about kidnapped girls? Aren't you happy Elizabeth is back?"

"Yes, of course I'm happy she is back safely, but I don't have the kidnapper. Unofficially, I'm not even sure she was kidnapped."

"Let's assume that she was kidnapped by the apes."

"So..."

"You solved the crime," said Alicia

"I don't have a criminal."

"Maybe there is no criminal."

"Can't have a crime without a criminal," said Habimana.

"Assuming the apes kidnapped Elizabeth, it's either a crime and Stone and his group are criminals, or it's not a crime and there are no criminals," said Alicia.

"Didn't we have this conversation before?"

"I'm trying to convince you that you did your job. You got Bee back. That was a crime, you caught the criminal and kicked her out of Rwanda. Now you got Elizabeth back. Just accept that her kidnapping was not a crime and there are no criminals. Or, go along with Kanoro's story and make the Chinese woman and her poachers the criminals in Elizabeth's kidnapping too."

"Maybe Ja helped."

"Your only eye witness cleared him."

"So what do you think?" asked Habimana.

"I think a being that could plan and carry out a girl's kidnapping is enough like a human to be charged with a crime," said Alicia.

"I never thought I'd hear you say that."

"It's even worse. Remember, one of the chimpanzees tried to sexually molest Elizabeth, and the same one assaulted me for no good reason. That's more criminal than the kidnapping. The chimpanzees even agreed, and they punished him."

"So, do I arrest the chimpanzees and punish them?"

"You would be saying that they are mentally capable of standing trial and defending themselves."

"Yeah, I guess so."

"Here's my problem. If chimpanzees are mentally competent to know right from wrong, to commit crimes, and be judged and punished by humans, then are they human?" asked Alicia. "Do they have the same rights as humans?"

"That would never fly in Rwanda and probably not in the rest of the world."

"You're right there. The philosophers talk about 'personhood'," said Alicia. "Some say that although chimpanzees are not human, they are enough like us to have 'personhood'. The philosophers then conclude that they have the legal right to be free and to be free of pain and persecution. One judge in New York has ruled that you don't have to be human to have personhood, but other courts and most people believe that chimpanzees really don't have all of the same rights and competencies as humans."

"If they do have rights, then wouldn't they also have responsibilities?" asked Habimana.

"That's where I fall apart. That's logically correct, but I just feel that it's wrong to judge them and punish them as we would humans. Mango was a bad apple. Maybe he was insane. If the chimpanzees hadn't killed him, we would have had to, eventually. He was a clear danger to people and he had to go."

"So being kidnapped was not dangerous to Elizabeth?"

"Some, but the apes were kind to her. They brought her food and bedding. They groomed her. Potato played with her. Elizabeth told me that Stone helped her get out of the cave, and that the chimpanzees brought her back to the road."

Habimana sat back in his chair and took a swallow of cold coffee. "Officially, we solved the crimes and caught the human criminals. They got off easily but they were punished."

"And-" began Alicia, but Habimana cut her off.

"Let me get this right. If the apes did kidnap Elizabeth, it was also a crime, we caught the criminals, but we decided not to punish them. You and I decided not to punish them. Maybe we are treating them as children or mentally handicapped people, who can't be held responsible for their actions."

"I'll settle for that."

"We should both be very happy that we got Bee back. What would have happened if we hadn't?"

Epilogue

Alicia completed her research and returned to Brazil where she wrote and successfully defended her doctoral thesis. She submitted several papers that were based on her thesis to scientific journals. They were accepted. She was living her dream. She visited Senhor Carvalho and checked on the progress of the golden lion tamarins, which were thriving and reproducing prolifically. Alicia once again declined Carvalho's proposal of marriage, and submitted a new grant proposal to return to Rwanda. This time she got her research visa before she arrived. She continued her study of the Gishwati chimpanzees and recruited a doctoral student to study the mountain monkeys. Alicia also mentored many Rwandan university students doing research on the plants and animals of Gishwati.

The Rwandan government made the Gishwati Forest Reserve into a national park, with an ecotourism program. The park included the Mukura Forest Reserve, which was another small forest that was 20 miles away. A commitment was made to plant a forest highway between Mukura and Gishwati so that the chimpanzees could expand their range. Batwa were hired to plant the trees. There were no chimpanzees in Mukura, but scientists were confident that the Gishwati group would eventually find their way there. Alicia proposed reintroducing a group of chimpanzee orphans to Mukura to speed the process and add needed genetic variety to the Gishwati group.

Elizabeth Weatherby eventually told her story. It was a sensation, but sensible people, including even Whitney

Logan, dismissed it as the romantic wanderings of a spoiled college girl who, perhaps, had suffered a head injury. Some suspected that she made up the story as a cover for her having run off for a brief fling with a muscular Rwandan in the Land of a Thousand Hills. Alicia and Peter decided not to publically corroborate her story. Alicia's career was too promising for her to discredit her scientific reputation with a kooky-sounding story that most of her colleagues could not believe. Peter did not want Gishwati to become a mecca for those with romanticized views about animal intelligence and emotion. He decided that Habimana was right: chimpanzees could be stolen but not kidnapped, killed but not murdered. Clay Cave became a cult destination for those who believed Elizabeth's story. Several tourists fell off the rock face while trying to get to the cave.

Madam Chen returned to Africa and set up a new illegal animal trade operation in Uganda, just north of the Rwandan border. INTERPOL had lost track of her during her deportation to China. She already had poachers scouting a small chimpanzee population in the Kyambura Gorge. Many, including Lieutenant Habimana, stuck to the official story that Madam Chen had orchestrated Elizabeth's kidnapping. According to this theory, Chen had Elizabeth returned to the Gishwati Forest when the police were closing in on her place in Gisenyi.

Gaslight International made a seven-figure donation to the Clinton Foundation for educational and economic improvement of the lives of rural residents of Rutsiro District in Rwanda. The centerpiece of the program was establishment of a school and community center in the Batwa village, with five-year contracts for a teacher and a social psychologist, both of whom had had extensive experience in rural Africa. The school offered courses on Kinyarwanda, English and the Batwa languages, arithmetic, and African and world history. Adults and children were separated at school so that the adults would not be demeaned by starting at the same competency levels as the kids. The community center provided experiences in farming, nutrition, sanitation, health, family planning, community relations, bee keeping, electronic banking, calendars and watches, and use of telephones and computers. A cooperative was formed to foster and organize the Batwa dance tradition. The dance troupe made an income by entertaining Gishwati visitors and was even invited to perform for H.E. in Kigali. Elizabeth Weatherby and Whitney Logan returned to intern at the school and center. Elizabeth was not among those who visited Clay Cave.

Bee grew up as Potato's adopted sister. Squash bravely nursed both for more than a year. Poachers did return to Gishwati, and Thistle got caught in a wire snare. The chimpanzees ripped up the tree to which the snare had been tied, but Thistle could only pull on the thick wire, and it dug ever more deeply into his wrist as he towed the tree through the forest. Bee used her new knowledge of slipknots to push on the wire and remove the snare. Other chimpanzees watched closely. No Gishwati ape would ever again be caught for long in a snare. Carrot, Bee, Thistle, and Potato would be the first Gishwati apes to arrive at Mukura.

Cat sought out Bee for play sessions for six more months. Potato was always excluded. After six months, Cat returned with a female and three serval kittens, which he introduced to the Gishwati chimpanzees with both pride and reservation. They joined Bee for some wrestling bouts, and Potato was allowed to play with the kittens. Ja was delighted by these six-way pile-ups, and they became a new metaphor in the Batwa oral tradition. Servals and chimpanzees were to live in peace in the Gishwati Forest, and Bee and Cat became satisfied with occasional glimpses of one another.

Peter was accepted by the University of Rwanda and graduated from its distinguished biology program with honors. Upon graduation, he was appointed as the warden of the Gishwati National Park. He organized a program by which Batwa women could enter the park and gather medicinal plants. He finally made Clay Cave off-limits to tourists as a matter of human safety and as a part of the natural heritage of both the chimpanzees and the Batwa.

Afterword: Getting Real

As I said in the Foreword, some of the descriptions of chimpanzee behavior and thinking in this story are based on documented scientific observations, and others are exaggerations that are not (currently) documented but are plausible, at least to me. What follows is an attempt to separate what is exaggerated from what has been scientifically documented. Space does not allow a list of references but an Internet search will help locate sources and their authors.

COMMUNICATION: The descriptions of chimpanzee communication by gesture, facial expressions, and sounds are scientifically based, with the exception of Stone's ability to communicate sets of instructions to other chimpanzees using gestures. There is also no evidence that Stone would have the conceptual ability to hang Alicia's boot on a tree as a form of apology, and no evidence that Stone could have communicated with Peter by exchanging the printout with his and Bee's pictures. It is true that chimpanzees and other apes do not cry or produce tears, but I know of no observations of chimpanzees wanting to lick human tears.

One of the most significant differences between chimpanzees and humans is that chimpanzees are not capable of speaking a language. Their mouths, tongues, throats, and lips do not allow them to form the sounds that people use to speak. Scientists have shown that apes have the brainpower to understand the meanings of many words and to communicate with words that are in the form of symbols on a computer screen or on a magnetic board, or with sign language. But chimpanzees are unlikely ever to discuss complicated, abstract issues such as personhood, or to write scientific papers.

FEEDING BEHAVIOR: The descriptions of eating flowers, fruits, and shoots are simplified but accurate. Hunting and killing monkeys by chimpanzees has not yet been observed at Gishwati but is documented among wild chimpanzees elsewhere. The snake-eating incident is based on unpublished observations that I and my colleagues made elsewhere in Rwanda. Chimpanzees are known to eat clay for its trace minerals.

SOCIAL BEHAVIOR: The descriptions of chimpanzee aggressive behavior (including male-male killing), dominance, grooming, food-sharing, sexual behavior, mother-infant and sibling relationships, and play among and between chimpanzees are based closely on scientific observations. The uncertainty about whether hunting by male chimpanzee groups is truly synchronized and cooperative is simplified but accurate. Chimpanzees have been known to "adopt" orphaned infants but they were not directed to do so by a dominant male.

NESTING: The descriptions of nests and nest-building are simplified but accurate. To my knowledge no chimpanzee has been observed to provide nesting material to or build a nest for another.

TOOL USE: The descriptions of the chimpanzees' use of leaf sponges and stone hammers are based many documented accounts, although these types of tools have not yet been observed to be used by the Gishwati chimpanzees. Although chimpanzees and other great apes use tools, they power them with their own strength and with gravity. They are unlikely ever to invent technological tools, such as helicopters and smartphones, that are powered by fossil fuels and electricity.

MEDICINAL PLANTS: There are scientific claims for the use of medicinal plants by chimpanzees, and in some cases the same plant is also used as medicine by people. I know of no descriptions of one chimpanzee providing medicinal plants to another or to a human.

CAVES: At least one chimpanzee population is known to use caves for shelter and cooling, but there is no account of them storing anything in the caves.

AGGRESSION TOWARD PEOPLE: Pet chimpanzees and chimpanzees in zoos and sanctuaries have been known to attack and even kill people. I know of no accounts of attacks on people by unprovoked wild chimpanzees. I know of no accounts of sexually-intended attacks on people by chimpanzees, but male orangutans have been known to try forcibly to undress women.

TRADING BY CHIMPANZEES: Great apes in zoos and laboratories are reliably reported to exchange items with people. The descriptions of trading by zoo apes in the story are factual, although most involved orangutans. My own experience with orangutans indicates that they can understand the value of items and adjust their trading strategies accordingly: really good items cost more. Chimpanzees are reported to exchange items with people and with other apes, even without being trained to do so. They are said to have a sense of fairness and reciprocity in their bartering. They have been trained to work for and then exchange tokens, which are virtually useless to them except as "money" that can be used to "buy" something they want. One experiment showed that they consistently "overpay." There is at least one study that shows that captive chimpanzees who share food with another individual are more likely to be groomed later by that individual. This implies that both parties remember the "deal" for some time. There is still uncertainty about whether food-sharing among wild chimpanzees results in later grooming, sexual access, or support in aggression. However, Stone's conceiving of and implementing the plan to exchange Elizabeth for Bee is clearly a leap of imagination. It's made a bit more credible by the return of the unconscious boy by the Brookfield Zoo gorilla, which is a true story. But chimpanzees and the other great apes probably lack the conceptual ability to conduct a kidnap-for-ransom, which is a trade or barter that is conducted over long distances and long time periods and involves considerable abstract thinking. You do not have to worry about being kidnapped or attacked by wild great apes if you have the chance to visit them.

PLAY AND FRIENDSHIP BETWEEN CHIMPANZEES AND OTHER ANIMALS: Individual animals are known to play and form "friendships" with individual animals of a different species. This is especially true of domestic animals and of animals in captivity. An orphan chimpanzee being raised in a sanctuary has recently been reported to have befriended a domestic cat. A laboratory gorilla did likewise. However, there is no evidence that two such different animals as Bee and Cat would form a lasting friendship with deep emotional ties and food-sharing.

MIRRORS: Captive and wild apes eagerly look into mirrors and other reflecting surfaces. At first, like human children, they react as if the reflected image is another, but they soon learn that the image is him- or herself. They groom themselves, and examine their teeth and other visually inaccessible body surfaces in the mirror. Captive chimpanzees who have had dye marks placed unobtrusively by experimenters on their foreheads (where they can't see the marks without a mirror) will touch the mark when they look into a mirror. Scientists regard mirror self-recognition as evidence that chimpanzees have a sense of self or self-awareness.

PHOTO RECOGNITION: Chimpanzees have been shown to be able to differentiate two-dimensional photographs of chimpanzees from other animals and objects. At least one chimpanzee has been shown to differentiate between photographs of individual chimpanzees and even match the names of individuals (chimpanzees and humans) to their photos. However, I am unaware of any evidence that suggests that Stone and the other Gishwati chimpanzees could recognize photographs of themselves and other group members without extensive practice at the task. There is also no scientific evidence that Stone could interpret Peter's red circle as an indication that he and Bee would soon be reunited.

UNDERSTANDING INTENTIONS: Chimpanzees have been shown scientifically to be able to understand what another, including a human, wants to do or is trying to do, and will actually help. Rain helping Elizabeth break sticks for Ja's splint, Stone's delivering food to Elizabeth in the cave or helping her climb up the riverbank or over the rockface are more complicated than any scientific observations to date, but they are quite plausible. Captive chimpanzees have been shown to cooperate with one another and with people to solve problems, and wild chimpanzees also comfort and show compassion to one another.

COMPASSION: Wild chimpanzees regularly console others who have been attacked or injured. They provide and share food with others, and groom others who are frightened or stressed. I have been consoled by a zoo orangutan when I was sad. However, I am unaware of any evidence that would suggest that an ape would provide food, nesting material, or comfort to a distressed human over an extended period of time.

GRIEF: Wild and captive chimpanzees have been documented to grieve for dead siblings and close associates. They become depressed, lose their appetites, stop playing, and sometimes even visit and view a body. Stone's expressions of grief upon Apple's death, and his grieving for the disappeared Bee are entirely plausible.

POACHING AND HUNTING APES: Chimpanzees are commonly hunted for food ("bushmeat") although not in Rwanda. When a mother is killed for food, her infant may be taken alive in the hope that she or he can be sold as a pet. Ape infants are sometimes specifically targeted for the pet trade, and their mothers and other group members who try to protect the infant are killed. This is becoming less common because international laws and treaties make it illegal and there is greater public awareness of the cruelty that is involved. But ape sanctuaries still receive infant apes that are orphaned by these practices.

SANCTUARIES AND REINTRODUCTION: The numbers of orphaned apes, the ways in which they become orphans, and their desperate psychological plight are accurately described. The dedication and skills of ape sanctuary staffs and veterinarians are well-documented. The accounts of attempts to reintroduce rehabilitated ape and gorilla orphans are also accurate. In reality, Bee, at 19 months of age, would probably be too young and too dependent on her mother to survive reintroduction, even with her adoption by Squash and protection by her older sister Rain and by Stone. I could have made Bee three or four years old, at which age she would be more likely to survive reintroduction, but Bee just "wanted" to be 19 months old and she was "determined" to survive.

SNARES: Poachers throughout Africa use slipknot snares to catch small- and medium-size mammals. Great apes are often caught in these snares. The apes are able to break the snare from the tree to which it is attached, but no wild ape has been documented to have learned how to remove a snare from an arm or leg. Many die gruesomely from infection, joint dislocation, and shock. Given enough time to "fiddle" with a snare, I am sure an ape could learn how to remove it, and they certainly could be trained to remove them. Gorillas have been documented to disable snares when they find them in the forest. But Bee's removal of the snare from

Cat's leg is an accomplishment that is undocumented.

Personhood and Ape Rights: The great apes are the living animals that are most closely related to humans, and, of all of the apes, chimpanzees are the most closely related to us. Some philosophers and legal experts have argued that chimpanzees are sufficiently human-like to deserve the same legal rights as humans living in democracies: freedom from unnecessary pain and punishment, freedom from unjustified captivity, freedom from unjustified death, freedom to move around freely and make responsible choices, and freedom of expression. This is called "personhood." But chimpanzees are not people and people are not chimpanzees. As noted in the Foreword, we have been evolving separately for about six million years. There are significant differences as well as significant similarities between chimpanzees and at least adult humans. Today, at least in the United States, apes are legally regarded as property, like a cow or a slave, but some legal scholars feel that they should be given the rights of legal personhood. The discussions about personhood and legal rights among Alicia, Peter, and Lieutenant Habimana accurately portray this yet-unresolved controversy. Words are important. Note that I use the pronoun "who" not "that" to refer to chimpanzees, i.e. "the chimpanzee who..." The use of "kidnap" rather than "steal" or "poach" and "murder" rather than "kill" in the dialogue are other examples where words indicate attitudes toward personhood.

Dear Reader,

You can help write the future of Gishwati!

The Forest of Hope Association is a Rwandan not-for-profit organization that is working with the Rwandan government to protect Gishwati and its chimpanzees and to improve the lives of people in the area. To learn more and to get the latest news on the establishment of the Gishwati National Park, see www.fharwanda.org

U.S. citizens can make tax-deductible contributions to the Forest of Hope Association through the Gishwati Foundation (www.gishwati.org).